PRAYERS FOR AN ANGEL

PAUL MANGANARO

CONTENTS

This book is dedicated to Karen, for her generous spirit in helping children with autism live in a bigger world.

CHAPTER 1. ARRIVAL OF THE OLD MAN. AUGUST

olks call me Poet. What I'm about to tell you happened not too long ago. I think somethin' like this must'a taken place so many times before, and may just happen again where you live someday. Just like in a play, each person took on a part, without even knowin' they were doin' it. This story's prob'ly played out in ev'ry city throughout the world for more than a couple thousand years now. But this time, the story had a dif'rent endin'. 'Cause this time, people *made* somethin' dif'rent happen.

sLike I was sayin' I'm called Poet, but not 'cause I use two-dollar words, and I sure don't talk in rhymes. Fact is, I make it my biz'ness to talk plain. I'm like a poet 'cause of my soul. I used to be nothin' but a cynic and a disbeliever, but inside, my heart always felt an ache for the hurtin' folks around me. If you'd'a met me before this all happened, I'd'a seemed like I didn't care. But ev'ry day I was lookin' for hope. Folks call me Poet 'cause my eyes see beauty and my ears hear the truth. My old heart beat tired and painful through the hardness of life, while at the same time, it was searchin' for the healin' powers of love.

It's somethin' that a country boy like me ended up spendin' so much time in cities. I've walked through cities all over this country from high to low. I used to live in a place for a while, 'til I learned the people in that place were no dif'rent from the folks in the last place I drifted from, then I'd move on again. Cement and steel buildin's are hard on the outside, and inside they can be full of life. That's the way I was. That's the way lots of folks in cities are. They still have life in 'em, no matter how hard livin' has made their outsides. I roamed all around, havin' hope that someday I'd find a cluster of folks with good hearts like mine, and there, I'd set myself down and grow roots. Then one day, there I was!

As I walked through life, I learned I had a choice. Either to hang my head down low, to see the garbage in the dark corners, or to lift my head upwards to look at the sky. Sometimes, the sky is so beautiful, I think God is right there behind it. Now that I know what I know, I choose to look across. Not up to see God, or down to see dirt, but across to see the other people like me. I'm dif'rent now that I crossed paths with the one other person who walked the deserts of the earth in search of a spring of clear water; a homeless stranger to ev'ryone. I'm a changed man today 'cause I met him.

I'd been in this one place for some time. It seemed like so many other cities I been in. You know the kind of place I mean: tall buildin's, cracks in the sidewalks, folks rushin' by – hurryin' to go places they don't want to get to. I expected I'd feel like movin' along again before long. But then, somethin' happened. And here's how it all started...

There was this one hot summer day in August. The kind of a day when the noonday sun heats the black streets soft. The kids were hangin' around in a group by Coen's Deli just before lunch like they always did. I'd been in town long enough to know their names. There were four of 'em. I'd stop and watch 'em play sometimes. Watchin' 'em, made me feel very young and very old at the same time. I knew those days of youth were long past for me, but their spirits made my heart beat so... makin' me wish I could turn the hands of time back to when I was young. Made me wonder what happened to all the kids I grew up with, wishin' I could go back to my hometown to see 'em all, just one more time.

Tryin' to think back to when I was young was like tryin' to see somethin' through a fog, but I tried to remember anyway. Old age is like that, always lookin' back. I remembered enough to know it was hard bein' a kid. They don't know the reason for the hard-edged games they play, but I do. I saw the older ones takin' the place of their parents by teachin' the young – toughenin' 'em up for what was ahead.

Sometimes a tender thing'll slip through the cracks but keeps on growin' anyway. Rough talk, a little shovin', a bit of bullyin', reminds the softest souls they'll be hurt 'less they let the calluses grow over. Today the kids were fightin' over a flower. A soft, fragile, little thing that grew from a crack in the sidewalk, on the side of Coen's store.

"Look at that," said the girl. That's Sam – short for Samantha. "It's a purple flower!"

"What's it doin' *there*?" said Vic. He asked without wantin' to hear an answer back. He's the oldest boy, at about twelve. A lost soul if there ever was one. 'Cause he didn't have a good home, he acted like he was drownin'; grabbin' at anything and ev'rything just to tread water. "That don't belong here," he said.

Dadge is the second oldest boy; about ten years old. He stepped in front of Vic to keep him from stompin' on the thing. He's generally quiet – like he's always thinkin'.

"Let it alone," Sam hollered. She's plucky. A regular fighter. Never once saw her wearin' a dress, and I'm sorry to say, hardly ever saw her wearin' a smile. "It's grown up this far, so you should let it alone!"

The littlest one ran up to Vic and started swattin' at him with somethin' that looked like on an old rag. Whatever it was, he never let go of it. Pauly's a lively, five-year-old with a brightness in his eyes that could light up a city block at midnight. The two older boys in the group had spent time coachin' him over the past several months to try to get him to fight for his place in the neighborhood. It was no use though… Pauly was as harmless as a pup.

"You heard Sam. Don't hurt it!" Pauly hollered.

"I don't think so," said Vic, pushin' him to the ground.

Sam and Dadge shoved hard to move Vic away from the flower. They kicked and punched, with Vic plowin' forward and laughin'. The flower was crushed before Pauly could get on his feet again to join back in the fight.

"That was mean. I wonder what kind of flower it was?" said Sam, lookin' at where the flower used to be.

"It was a *purple* flower," said Pauly.

"Maybe it will grow back again," said Dadge.

It was then, when I saw the sadness in 'em, I heard myself say outloud: "I wish things could be better for them, then they were for me."

Like I was sayin', I thought this was just goin' to be like ev'ry other place I'd been. But I was wrong because of what happened next.

I'll never forget the first time I saw the old man. He appeared like a vision made mystic by the waves of heat risin' from the broilin' street. All the color in his hair went out years ago, leavin' only pure white behind. His uncombed hair flowed over his ears, touchin' the tops of his shoulders. White stubble sprouted out of his face, just long enough to make the beginnin's of a beard.

His clothin', a terrible mismatch of random finds, colored his lanky body like a homemade patchwork quilt. A tie-dye tee-shirt, khaki green shorts, one navy blue sock, one black. His socks were pulled up high on his calves above his red sneakers. He leaned on the handle of his upright cart. Two wheels, big as plates, were the foundation of the rectangular cage. Some old handbells, all dif'rent from one another, hung on the outside of the cart and jingled while he walked.

As I watched him come toward me, I wondered if the cart he pushed was there to hold junk that was in it, or if he was usin' the thing to steady himself like a walker. The bars makin' up the cart were shiny chrome. Beams of sun bounced off the metal, sendin' rays of light across the paths of pedestrians walkin' by.

A head would turn and trace the light back to the old man, and quickly turn away again. Without missin' a step, the distracted lookers would continue their rush forward in this, another day in the human race.

The man's eyes were fixed. His look passed by me over my right shoulder. He focused on the doorway I was standin' next to. I could hear the wheels of his cart squeak as he got close, and I heard a couple of the bells ringin'. Then he stopped in front of the store that was caddy-corner across the street. As he stood there, starin' at the store I was standin' in front of, a look of satisfaction came over him. Like a weary traveler who found his long-awaited oasis. I could see him readin' the sign overhead: 'Coen's Corner: Kosher Delicatessen est. 1976'. It was right next door to Amir's Tobacco shop. The delicatessen had been there for decades but not near as old as the buildin' it was set into.

Maybe it's 'cause folks don't *want* to see somebody whose troubles are too many to be fixed. That's not the way it was for me. I felt like the whole city was under a spell and that *I* was the only one able to see him 'cause of some kind'a magic – like I was priv'leged. I watched the old man, as he crossed over toward Coen's.

The kids had settled down and were all millin' around in front of the store gettin' ready for their lunches. The four castoffs had been together long before I came to town. Up 'til now, they'd stuck together, but things were about to change. With a screech of brakes, the kids turned to look. Pauly was the first of 'em to notice the dog.

"The dog! It's gonna get hit by the car!" Pauly yelled. He tugged on Vic's shirt like he was ringin' a bell. He was lookin' up at him yankin', callin' Vic to action. A big mutt with long, brown, hair staggered down the center of the busy street. It was almost a block away from Coen's and headin' straight toward the old man. Vic's long reach grabbed Pauly's shoulder stoppin' him in his tracks.

"Don't go near it. That dog has the rabies," Vic said.

"What's the rabies?" asked Pauly.

"It means, that dog's crazy, and if it bites you – you die," said Vic.

"How do you know it has the rabies?" asked Sam.

Sam was the local tomboy. Rough and tough as a girl of eight could be. Her eyebrows were always low. Like they were carved onto her face by pure determination. She kept up with Dadge, the second to the oldest boy in the group. Her short hair was no disguisin' that she was a girl. Under the rustled blonde hair and a little dirt was a bud, a few years away from bloomin' into a prize flower.

"Maybe it's sick, and that's why it's walkin' funny," said Dadge, lookin' to Vic for some wisdom.

Dadge was tall for a boy of ten. He looked older than he was, but there was no doubt in my mind he was still a boy. His straight brown hair hung down from not being tended to. He was growin' out of his clothes, prob'ly waitin' for the next batch of hand-me-downs to come his way.

It was then, when the four kids were lookin' at the dog, that they saw the old man walkin' diagonally across the street toward Coen's. The man had heard the car skid too, and stopped short of the curb. Changin' course, he set his cart in front of Coen's, reached out his arms, and headed straight toward the mutt.

"That old man's gonna get bit," said Vic. "He's as crazy as that dog!"

"Maybe he wants to help the dog," said Sam.

"I wouldn't go near a rabies dog," said Vic. "If I had a gun, I'd shoot it!"

From the midst of all the talkin', and yellin', a quiet voice broke through as the old man spoke. His words were sure and steady as a cool breeze to the overheated mutt. As he talked to the dog, I felt the peace in his voice.

"Everything's going to be alright, boy. Come to me. I'll help you," he said.

I should'a called out to him. To stop him from messin' with the dog. I felt bad for reactin' so slow. But, by the time I thought of it, the dog was right in front of him; its dry tongue hangin' low. He said somethin' else to the dog I couldn't hear 'cause now he was almost a half a block away. One hand took hold of the collar, while the other patted the dog's head. Then he turned back around and started leadin' the dog toward us.

"I'm leavin'!" Vic yelled. "*I'm* not gettin' bit."

Mrs. Coen heard Vic's yellin' and hurried outside.

"What happened?" she shouted to the back of Vic's head as he took off down the street.

"That old man's crazy!" he hollered, not lookin' back.

Vic turned the corner and was out of sight. Gray-haired Mrs. Coen, ('Leah' as I call her), was parent to any child who let her mother 'em. She was short and mostly round. She was friendly and looked like she needed kids to hug her.

"What's the matter, Dadge?" she asked with her Yiddish accent. "Why did Vic run away?"

"It's because that crazy old man's bringing that dog with rabies over here," he said pointin'.

The old man led the dog right up to our corner, stoppin' short of the curb. Seem's the spell had changed some by then. Now, the kids *and* Leah could see the man. Felt like the entire population walked by, not lookin' at all, as if the old man and the dog were invisible to ev'rybody but us.

Sam and Dadge backed away, pro'bly 'cause of Vic's cautions. But not Pauly. Leah held Pauly close by her side to stop him from reaching out to pet the dog. Leah and I looked at each other for a while. I was makin' up my mind whether the dog and the man were safe to go near. I figured she was doin' the same. Finally, we gave each other a look and she let the boy go. Pauly shot straight toward the man.

"Some water, please," the old man said to us, steppin' onto the curb. "It's not for me. It's for the dog."

"I'll get a water bottle," said Pauly.

The man walked up in front of the doorway of the deli and stopped, still holdin' on to the dog's collar. Pauly ran inside, behind the counter and ripped away some of the plastic wrappin' from the case, pullin' out a warm bottle of water, then he scurried back outside.

"Here!" said Pauly, smilin' up at the old man holdin' the bottle up.

"Thank you, young man. My new friend is thirsty."

The man got down on his knees in front of the dog and poured some water into his cupped hand. The dog lapped it up like he needed it bad.

"How did you know the dog wasn't going to bite you?" asked Sam.

"I didn't think he would hurt me. When I looked into his eyes, I could see he needed a friend."

Sam stood a good bit away, watchin' the dog drink from the man's hand, tryin' to figure out if it was safe to get any closer.

"The man's right, Sam," I said. "The dog wouldn't drink water if it had the rabies."

After I said that, Sam got up next to Pauly and started strokin' the dog too.

"Look on his tag and see who he belongs to," said Leah. "Maybe the owner is worried."

Sam fished around on the collar and said, "It's gone," holdin' up the ring where the tag used to be.

I felt the ring to be sure my eyes hadn't lied. Then I told 'em, "The ring looks like it's been worked over by plyers. This dog isn't lost. He's been dumped here."

"I believe that's so," said the old man.

"I have money," said Pauly, holdin' out a few coins he had. "He looks hungry."

"You're right. Of course, he's hungry," said the man. "Too much water won't be good for him right now."

"Save your money, Pauly. I'll get it this time," I said. "Guess the dog needs to eat like the rest of us."

Dadge had stepped in close to the dog by this time, feelin' brave since we all reckoned the dog was safe.

"Come on in with me and get a paper plate," I said to Dadge, "so the food doesn't make a mess on the sidewalk."

Dadge rushed into the store after me. I set the can of dog food on the counter and was reachin' in my pocket for the money when Dadge ran by snatchin' it away.

"I'll feed him," he said, paper plate in hand. "Just in case he bites."

"When you're done feeding the dog, come back inside. It's time for you children to eat lunch now," said Leah.

The lunch crowd was always thick at the deli. It started up well before noon ev'ry day. Besides Leah and her husband, Max, the Coens needed two workers to fix lunches for customers. I generally showed up about noon, 11:30, if I wanted to socialize, that's when the kids got their lunch sandwiches. Leah'd give 'em another batch later in the day, to make sure they had somethin' to eat for dinner.

Pauly and Sam watched the dog lap up the food, while Dadge went and stood by the display case watchin' Leah make their sandwiches. The stranger stood by Pauly and Sam out front, watchin' the dog eat, lookin' pleased as punch. I struck up a conversation with him to see what he had to say.

"I haven't seen you around before," I said, makin' sure my voice sounded friendly. "Just get into town?"

"Yes, I did. I arrived this very day. I'm from up north."

"Folks call me 'Poet'".

"My name's Engle. My first name is Himmel, but you can call me Hi."

He stuck his hand out to shake. I pretended like I didn't see. I wasn't goin' to shake hands with someone I hadn't figured out yet.

"I've been here a while myself," I said. "Don't guess you've had time to find a place to stay yet."

"I'd like to find a place as soon as I can. I'd hate to leave all my things outside overnight and have them get damaged."

"I can point you in the right direction in findin' a place."

Now that I was close up, I looked him over real good. He was scrubbed clean as far as I could tell. His clothes looked clean too. Somehow, even with all that cleanliness, he sure was a mess. As for the things in his cart – didn't look to me like the rain could hurt 'em one bit.

"I didn't pass any gas stations on my way in. I suppose I'll end up pushing broom or washing dishes."

"You'll need more money than a job like pushin' broom will get you for a place around here."

"Oh, I understand. I have friends who'll send my Social Security check along as soon as I get settled. The sooner I find a place the better. Do you think there's a rooming house that allows dogs around here?"

"I don't know about any rooming houses, but I can show you a reasonable enough place where you can get a whole apartment."

"That would be wonderful!" he said. Then he looked down at the dog. "You want to come home with me, don't you?" he asked the dog.

The dog had already wolfed down the can of food. It looked up at Hi and barked when he heard 'home'.

"Home," repeated Hi. "You know what home means, don't you?"

The word 'home' raised the dog's spirits. He jumped up puttin' his paws on Hi's chest, lickin' his face.

"Home. We're going home!"

Hi kept repeatin' the word over and over. The dog stood on his hind legs barkin', lookin' like he was jumpin' for joy.

"Look at the way he's jumping. That's his name," said Hi.

"He's a dancer if I ever saw one. Your name is Dancer. From now on you're Dancer."

"What's going on here!" Max yelled; his voice, puttin' the brakes on the festivities. "You know I don't want people blocking the door, especially at lunchtime. Get away from the door!" he hollered as he came out of the deli. He delivered an extra, "Get away" to Hi and the dog. "I hope you're not giving food away to dogs now too!" he blustered to his Mrs. "It's bad enough you give free food away to these kids. Now maybe you're feeding stray dogs also?"

"*I* bought the can of food Max," I told him. "You know I always pay my way."

I knew Max for a while by then, and didn't pay attention to his hollerin', neither did the kids for that matter. As far as I could tell, he was nothin' but an old lion without any teeth. No matter if he was yellin' or just talkin', I loved to listen to him. To my ears, his Yiddish accent made his voice sound like music from another country.

"Get everyone from in front of the store," he kept on. "How can we do business with this menagerie blocking the doorway?" Then Max, who was almost as old as Hi, looked up toward heaven sayin'; "This old man is doing circus tricks with a dog no less. Is this supposed to be an attraction?" After that, Max talked right to Hi. "You should move with your dog to another street, please. Go, before you chase away all our trade."

"Come on children," said the missis. "Come away from the door. Mr. Coen is right. It's time for your lunches anyway. Come in."

I didn't get a free sandwich. Mrs. Coen had a soft spot

where kids were concerned, but not for a man like me, a senior, almost as old as her Max. She gave me my one and only free sandwich the first day I met her, and that was it. An old drifter like me wasn't entitled to any more handouts by her rules. I will say, she *has* been makin' my sandwiches mighty thick lately though. Max tolerated the store goods bein' given away to the kids, 'cause of the love he had for his wife. Leah had a heart of gold. Max was a dif'rent story. After the dust settled, he was back in the store behind the counter.

"Hey Mr. C.," said Dadge, "how about a ham sandwich?"

"This is a kosher delicatessen. There's no ham here. How many times do I have to tell you?"

Max sure sounded annoyed. It was only about the hundredth time Dadge asked him for a ham sandwich.

"If you'd get ham in here, you could sell a lot more sandwiches."

"Not in a million years. God wouldn't like it."

"Maybe God never *ate* a ham sandwich."

"Don't bother me or you'll find yourself outside!"

Max wasn't near as angry as he made out. I think he yelled just to keep his standing in the community as a curmudgeon. He could be real grumpy when he wanted to – and even sometimes when he didn't want to.

"Every day you come in here asking for a ham sandwich, and every day it's the same answer. Be thankful for what you get. If it was up to me, you'd get *no* sandwich!"

Leah's voice was a lot easier on the ears. "Here, Sam," she said from behind the display case of cold cuts. "Run and give this sandwich to that old man. Tell him it's for saving the dog from getting hit by a car."

By this time, Max and Leah were busy puttin' sandwiches together for their regular lunch crowd customers. Many of 'em went back two or even three decades to a time when Max was cheerful. Hard to believe when you're young and strong that somethin' could happen to knock a person so far off course. I didn't know at the time what had changed him. But since I'm tellin' you the story after it all happened, I'm gonna tell you ev'rything so you'll understand why.

I had followed Hi back into the street 'cause of what he said about needin' a place to stay. It was a chance for me to make a few dollars. Sam went runnin' up to us with Pauly trailin' right behind. He followed Sam around like a chick follows a mother hen.

"Here, mister," she said, tryin' her best to rustle up a smile for the old man. "It's from Mrs. Coen. She gives lots of people sandwiches. She said it's for saving the dog from being hit by a car."

"Thank you, young lady. Be sure to thank Mrs. Coen for me; that's very nice of her," he said smilin' back. "Tell me, what's your name?"

"It's Samantha, but everyone calls me Sam."

"Samantha's a beautiful name. I like the name, Sam, too."

"I'm Pauly," he said shy, hidin' half his face with the old rag.

"Hello, Pauly. I'm glad to meet you. And what do we have here?" he asked, bendin' down to get a closer look at what Pauly had in his clutches.

"It's Half-a Bear," Pauly said smilin', holdin' up the rag for the man's approval.

"It *was* a stuffed bear," Sam explained. "He carried it around so much the cloth ripped and let the stuffing out."

"I'm good at fixing broken toys. Would you let me put stuffing back in your bear for you?" he asked the boy.

"No," Pauly said, holdin' the bear up to his face and peekin' out with one eye. "I *like* him this way."

"He won't let *me* stuff it either. He never lets go of it. It's like his security blanket," said Sam. "When the stuffing started coming out, I told him it looked more like half a bear. So now he calls it Half-a Bear."

"I see. That's a good name for your bear."

"What's your name?" Pauly asked.

"I'm Mr. Engle."

"Mr. Angel," said Pauly, talkin' into Half-a Bear.

"Tell me, Sam, what do you want for Christmas?"

"It's August!" she said and burst out laughin' like Hi didn't know it was summer. "It's nowheres near Christmas time."

"I like Christmas so much; I start to think about it in June. It takes me months to get ready for it. Do you know what you want?"

"I usually don't get anything. Not unless Dadge gives us something. Then it's only candy or something like that."

"Well, I want you to think about what you want. And when you do, you'll tell me, won't you?"

"I guess. Gotta get back to the store. Time to get our sandwiches. Bye."

Sam and Pauly hurried back to the store. I saw Sam turn and stop. She gave Hi a strange look while shakin' her head.

"Now, why'd you do that?" I asked real angry. "Why get the kid's hope up for a Christmas present when her mother isn't gonna get her anything? 'Less you think she's gonna turn her trick money into Christmas gifts, instead of payin' rent so she can get thrown out in the snow."

"I'm not getting her hopes up without a reason. Christmas is a magical time of year where wishes come true."

"Listen! That kid's had her heart broken a million times, all the kids Leah feeds have. They all hang around together 'cause they're more family to each other than their own blood kin. You be careful how you treat 'em!"

"You don't understand," Hi said smilin' back at me.

I didn't want to hear him, so I just kept plowin' forward.

"I think the sun must'a gotten to you just like it got to that dog. If you *do* get a place, be sure it has cold water so you can stick your head in it."

Hi was takin' the verbal beatin' I was lashin' out, so, I let him have some more since I was on a roll.

"And by the way, notice there's only one sandwich. I didn't get one 'cause Leah only gives *one* of 'em away to men like us. So don't expect a handout tomorrow or any other day!"

It was like talkin' to cardboard. He acted like he didn't hear me yellin' at him. He stood there patient, with a pleasant smile, waitin' for me to let it all out. I didn't know what to make of him. Then he said:

"I'll save my sandwich for later." He said it real polite. "Mrs. Coen is such a special person. I wish there were more people with hearts like hers. Tell me, Poet, do you live in the same apartment building you mentioned?"

"Never mind where I live. Come on. I'll take you to the place I told you about. I'm not sure I ever want to see you again. I'm particular who I associate with. I spend *my* spare time tryin' *not* to talk to crazy people, so don't be surprised if you never see me after today!"

Lookin' back, I was awfully hard on him. Back then, I was the last one to think about buyin' a Christmas present for anybody. I never should'a talked that way. It wasn't that I was angry with Hi, so much as I was angry with ev'ry one of the parents of those kids. They were all good kids. Those parents were fools not to understand, they could'a had the best time in the world if they'd only spent time with their own. And maybe I was angry, 'cause I saw myself in 'em. I could see it on 'em sometimes, how their hearts hurt like mine did when I was a kid. How I wished things could'a been dif'rent for 'em, 'cause I knew how much it could hurt.

"I don't want you to be mad," said Hi. "I didn't ask for anything for myself, only some water for Dancer. You may think I'm not in my right mind because I helped a stray dog. Well, I like to help stray people too. That Mrs. Coen is a gem... She gives love to those children. She has even more to give, but her husband won't accept it. I'd like to help him, too. To be offered love is even rarer than being offered water in this world."

"You're damn straight about that! I get so tired of folks lookin' away when I walk toward 'em. Love! Folks won't even say hello to you these days. They'll look across, down, sideways, but never right at me. Like they're ashamed about the way they feel, about someone who doesn't have as much as they do."

After I said that about other people, I realized, I couldn't look *Hi* in the eye. His eyes shined so bright. As bright as the gleamin' rays that were bouncin' off his metal cart. I felt so small complainin' to him, when he had done somethin' good for the dog, and didn't have a bad thing to say about anything or anybody.

"Poet, I think most people are afraid," he went on. "They're afraid to reach their hand out for fear of getting it slapped. If they let their hearts lead them, they would believe holding your hand out, sometimes is the only way to get somebody else to reach back. I believe that most people would help if they thought the help they gave was permanent. You've probably heard it put something like; it's better to teach a person to fish instead of giving them spare change."

"I won't waste my time helpin' people," I said, "or give 'em anything either. Most folks would rather steal the shirt off your back before they'd give you their own. I protect what little I have. I'm not givin' my stuff away to the first person who has their hand out."

It was like his piercin' eyes were mirrors, shinin' my own self back at me. I heard my own words come right back. I had been sayin' things like that for as long as I can remember. I always thought I should'a had more. But when I said 'em this time, the words echoed back at me. His words rang true like one of the silver bells on his cart. My words echoin' back at me sounded lonely and empty. But there was no way I was goin' to let this old man change the way I think.

That's what I thought as I walked with Hi and the dog. It's what I thought as we passed in front of a woman. She was about ninety, I guess. She balanced crooked on the bones of her legs, all bent over and crippled. Her gnarled fingers looked like dry tree roots growin' around the top of her cane. The bones of her back stuck out so spiny, it made me hurt to look at her.

Shufflin' along the sidewalk with such caution, she was a fragile antique that might shatter into a million pieces if she took a fall. She turned her head away from studyin' the path before her and looked me right in the eye – givin' me a smile. I looked back in wonder and turned away feelin' ashamed of myself for bein' afraid to give her a smile in return.

I stopped listenin' to the old man as he chattered on about generosity and helpin' folks and such things. I thought he walked with dignity and spoke real proper. I was angry that woman was walkin' along that day, just as I was thinkin' about how I thought I should'a had more. There I was, up in age, with nothin' much to show for it. Folks here an' there had told me about God and how he works. I wouldn't believe 'em.

"I'm not goin' to believe that lady was there that day, at that time, to smile at me; a woman who should'a been cryin' and complainin' about bein' in pain and so close to her last days. What she got to be happy about anyway?" I thought.

"Am I supposed to think God made her leave her place at a certain time – that he planned out the course of our two lives so our paths would cross just then? Am I supposed to believe that he sent me on an errand with a crazy old man and that God timed it just right so that lady would smile at me just then?" I wasn't goin' to buy that.

That's what I thought that day as we walked up to the apartment buildin'. That's what I thought then... 'cept for the fact that I couldn't help thinkin' that woman's smile *was* meant for me. 'Cause it did somethin' to me. It changed me. I started to think, 'Why *did* I believe I didn't have enough, when I had so much more than so many others.'

"Well, Hi, here's the place I told you about. If you have a few dollars, you can get an apartment. Hot and cold runnin' mice and plenty of air conditionin'. The wind blows through this place in the winter like the buildin' wasn't even there. If it's nothin' else, it's affordable."

It was an old apartment buildin' made of red brick with tan stone windowsills. The sort of place that rich folks could live in someday if it was ever fixed up. They'd have to pay a small fortune to have the cement put back in between ev'ry brick again. It would need new windows, too. There was hardly a flake of paint on the wood frames and the glass that wasn't cracked or broken rattled in the wind like so many tin cans rollin' downhill. An optimist might call it the world's biggest wind chime.

The heavy front door creaked on its iron hinges. As we entered in, hot air hit our faces from inside the buildin'. Hi followed me up the stone steps haulin' his cart. The bells hangin' on the cart jingled as it thudded on each step he climbed. Hi was lean, but he was strong. I looked down into the cart. The stuff inside looked like an assortment of broken junk all of which seemed dumpster ready to me. Dancer followed behind – sittin' down ev'ry time Hi stopped, as if the old man had been his master for many years.

"Wait here for me, Dancer," Hi said, not like commandin' a dog, more like talkin' to a friend. "We won't be long." Dancer sat there pantin' in the heat.

The hallway walls had been painted, prob'ly when the buildin' was new. I couldn't tell what color it was before it turned dingy from neglect. It looked yellow/tan against the white parts of plaster where the walls had cracked and paint had fallen off. I knocked on apartment 1A. The knock bounced off the hard walls and tile floor. The TV from inside went quiet, then we heard a groan. It was the sound of a lazy man bein' dragged away from the comfort of his pastimes – eatin', drinkin', and reclinin'. The uneven footsteps of the landlord paced out a slight limp. We heard 'em over the sound of a couple of old box fans. The poundin' of the floor got louder as he walked up to the door.

Metal locks unlocked and a chain slid off. The old glass doorknob turned. An older man in his fifties with uncombed, baldin', dark hair stood lookin' bothered to no end. He dressed like I imagined many other landlords of this district were attired: a stained, white, sleeveless tee-shirt, light blue shorts, and black socks. Black, curly hair sprouted in clusters on his chest like ugly shrubs.

"Oh, it's you, Poet. You got another one for me?"

That's what I wanted to hear. That meant I was in for ten percent of the first month's rent for bringin' in a payin' tenant. It was like a code Jake and I had worked up together – months ago.

"That's right, Mr. Maschio. I've brought you another tenant. I'd like you to meet Mr. Engle."

"Himmel. You can call me Hi," he said, holdin' out his hand in friendship.

"Jake," he replied, *not* extendin' his hand. "So, you want a place? I got a place on the seventh floor. There's no air condi-tioning in the building. No elevator either. It's a walk-up."

They agreed on a price, meanin' Jake told him how much

the rooms were, and Hi said alright. I didn't know what the rooms looked like. I guess Hi needed a place real bad. Personally, I'd rather get rained on than stay in a dump like that.

"Pay your rent on time or I keep your stuff. No selling drugs out of the apartment. No cooking either. This is a safe place. Nobody's ever been killed here."

Hi was cheerful and polite the whole time and paid him some money. Jake gave me a wink before shuttin' the door.

"I'm not walkin' up there," I said. "I'd'a looked at it before I agreed to it if it was me. If you want to buy somethin' sight unseen, that's your business."

It was refreshin' to go out into the 90-somethin' degree heat again after bein' roasted alive in that buildin'. I could only imagine it got hotter as the floors went up.

"Come on, Dancer. We're almost home!"

Dancer walked quickly through the front door when he heard his master's voice. I wondered how a stray dog could'a known his name after such a short time, and then I took off right away. I decided to go back another day to collect my cut when Hi wasn't there. It wasn't much money anyway. How those two creatures could climb all those stairs to the seventh floor in that heat was not my worry.

That night I had a dream that bothered me. It wasn't a nightmare exactly, but the dream troubled me all the next day. I dreamed I was drivin' on a long, straight highway. I felt like it was important that I had to get someplace, but I didn't know where. There were lots of cars on the highway 'cause it was rush hour. I was comin' up to a bridge. It was one of those bridges that has cables holdin' it up. Traffic was gettin' backed up, so I drove onto the shoulder. When I got to the bridge, I started drivin' up the cables, like it was a road. That's the way dreams can be sometimes. Strange things can happen that don't make any sense. Climbin' higher and higher on the cables, I kept lookin' out of my car to see the river far below. The higher I went, the steeper the car climbed. I drove straight up after a while and felt like my car was gonna fall over backwards with me in it.

All the next day I wondered why I dreamed that dream and what it was all about. I hadn't driven a car since I was a young man. It wasn't until about mid-afternoon when I started to understand. I never got to where I was goin' in the dream. The closer I got to where I was goin', the more afraid I was. After I thought a little more, I knew that I had never gotten anywhere in life. I didn't think of myself as someone who was scared. On the other hand, gettin' someplace, or achievin' somethin' was never on my list of things to do. Seein' the brightness in Hi's eyes and watchin' him smile while Jake was takin' his money made me dream this somehow.

It was about a week later when I saw Hi again. I found out afterwards, the kids had a brush with him before then. They told me all about it, when it was all over a few months later, after Hi was gone for good.

CHAPTER 2. THE CROSSROAD – BRUSH WITH HI. AUGUST

The kids were all out in the park kickin' an old soccer ball around. It was mostly Dadge and Sam doin' the kickin'. They were tryin' to get Pauly to learn to kick straight. Vic was bored; too old to play like that anymore. He wandered away on purpose, toward a hill of boulders where older kids hung out. There were always some teenagers there ready to sell you somethin', or get you involved in some kind'a trouble. It's a sure thing that a bee will go to honey. It's also true, that young people without adults around to help 'em along, can be tempted to go down a dangerous path.

"Hey Vic," one of the teens called to him. "Hey man, it's Raphael. Remember me?"

Vic saw two teens talkin' to each other. One was Raphael, a tall guy about fourteen. He had a black baseball cap on sideways, sunglasses to look cool, and a black tee-shirt with a gold chain hangin' on the outside. Had a gold ring, and new lookin' slashed up jeans. He heard Raphael say low to the other guy, "He's okay."

The other guy was older, about sixteen. He stood next to Raphael with his hands on his hips, stickin' his chin out like he was darin' the world to take a swing at him. He was a short stocky kid, loaded down even more than Raphael, with gold chains and gold rings with diamonds in 'em. He was dressed in black with the same kind'a black baseball cap on.

"Remember me from school?" asked Raphael.

Vic was close now and could see Raphael's missin' front tooth. Vic figured it was from a fight.

"Oh yeah. I haven't seen you in a while. Where you been?"

"I dropped out. School is for suckers. This here's Ant'ny."

"Hey man," said Vic, holdin' out his fist.

Anthony stood there, still as a statue. Vic waited for Anthony to bump fists with him, but he didn't. After nothin' happened, Raphael fist-bumped with Vic.

"Hey, what'a you doin' hangin' around with those kids for? What are you, their babysitter?" Anthony asked, laughin'.

"Hey man, we're just playin' around."

"You like playin' with little kids?" Anthony said, goadin' him again.

"Wouldn't you like to score some of this instead?" Raphael asked, holdin' up his chain with his ring pointin' right in Vic's face. "How do you like *this*?"

Then Anthony reached in his pocket and pulled out a wad of bills, just about pushin' it in Vic's face.

"Six hundred bucks for doin' nothin'," he said. "What do you got in your pockets?"

"How'd you make that much?"

"Doin' stuff for a guy," said Anthony. "You want in?"

"Maybe. What I have to do to get that?"

"You gotta work up to it," said Anthony. "First, you gotta show me you can do somethin'. There's this guy in our territory runnin' a game he shouldn't. Sellin' fake CDs. All's you have to do is smash up his stuff. We gotta send him a message. Think you can do that?"

"What do I get out of it?"

Anthony punched him in the face and pushed him to the ground.

Vic was mad as a hornet, but Raphael held him down.

"Don't, Vic!" Raphael said.

"You get in!" Anthony yelled. "That's what you get! Make up your mind. You wanna get in or *not*?"

Raphael shook him some to be sure Vic wasn't goin' to fight back.

"Yeah. Okay." Vic said, wipin' off his face. Raphael held out his arm. Vic grabbed a hold of it and pulled himself up.

"You go to this address tonight," said Anthony, handin' him a wadded-up piece of paper. "Wait around until the guy leaves, then break in and smash everything. And don't get caught! You do, and you mention my name, I'll kill you!"

"Okay," Vic said, "but I gotta break in?"

"You got a problem with that?"

"No Ant'ny," said Raphael. "He can do it."

"Yeah, no problem," said Vic.

"Be here tomorrow, same time. Show me pictures of the broken shit, and I'll let you know how you did."

"Tomorrow, sure," said Vic.

"Don't mess up," Raphael said to him under his breath. "I told him you was okay."

Raphael and Anthony went back talkin' together as Vic went back to join the others. Dadge kicked the soccer ball to him. Vic gave it a quick kick back.

"I don't feel like playin'," he said to Dadge. "Get over here. I got somethin' to tell ya."

Dadge came over. Vic leaned in to talk private with him. "Meet me tonight by Coen's at eight. You gotta help me with somethin'. Be there! Don't let me down," he said and walked away.

Dadge nodded and went back to playin' with Sam and Pauly.

"What's up with him?" asked Sam.

"I don't know," replied Dadge. "He got all serious and left. Said he needs my help for somethin'."

"You watch him, Dadge," Sam warned. "He hasn't been the same lately. He's been hanging around with some rough kids. You be careful."

"Don't worry Sam. I'm no fool."

Dadge went on playin' but his heart wasn't in it anymore. He was worried about sayin' yes to somethin' when he didn't even know what it was.

CHAPTER 3. BREAKIN' UP CDS.
AUGUST

*I*t was still light out at eight. August was half over so ev'nin' was edgin' in quicker than usual. Vic stood by Coen's on the side of the buildin' where the flower had been crushed. His foot was shakin' from bein' nervous. He looked around for Dadge and was watchin' out for ev'ryone, as guilt would have it, as if the eyes of the world were on him.

"Hey, Vic!" Dadge called as he got near.

"Shut up man! Be cool."

"What's that for?" Dadge asked, lookin' toward the pry bar hangin' from Vic's hand. "You gonna kill somebody?"

"Don't be an asshole. I gotta do somethin' and you're comin' with me."

The look on Vic's face was enough to crush Dadge's good mood. He didn't joke after that. The boys walked together for a while, 'til they could hide in the shadows of night. Then Vic led Dadge to the address scribbled on Anthony's paper. They went around the back of the buildin' on the ally side, and hid behind some garbage pails, and waited. The alley was deserted so it was real quiet.

"What cha gonna do, Vic?" Dadge kept his voice down, mostly out of fear. "You're not really gonna kill somebody are you?"

"We're not killin' anybody. When this guy leaves, we're going in. He's in there now. See the light's on? You can see somebody movin' around in there."

The two glued their eyes to the windows of the room. It was a cinderblock addition, about twenty-foot square, in back of an old wooden buildin'. Shades were drawn, but they could see the shadow of a tall man walk across the windows now and then. They knew somethin' was goin' on in there. A few minutes before ten, they heard the door. The light went out and the man locked the back door and headed away.

"Now? Are we goin' in now?" Dadge asked.

"Wait. I wanna make sure he ain't comin' back."

Soft walkin' cats and car engines kept the two on edge 'til Vic gave the word.

"Follow me."

Vic fumbled with the pry bar, not knowin' how to use it. He jammed it in the door tryin' to get it open.

"Cut the screen with it," said Dadge, scoldin' Vic for doin' the wrong thing.

Vic sliced the screen with the bar and reached in through, unlockin' the simple latch from the other side. He cut his arm while reachin' in and hid it from Dadge.

"Now use the bar. Like this!"

Dadge jammed the bar in between the door jam and the old wood door. Then Vic took over, leanin' into it. He pushed his body down hard against the bar 'til he heard wood splinter. The door cracked open, and they were in.

Vic flicked on the switch and checked the place out. It was a one-man factory for makin' CDs. There was a printer with blank inserts next to a trimmer. They saw two machines for makin' copies and a few hundred blank CDs.

"What do we do now?" asked Dadge.

"This!" said Vic.

Swingin' the bar, he brought it down hard on the printer, smashing it a few more times 'til it was turned to junk. Then he slammed down on a few piles of CDs watchin' the case pieces go flyin'.

"Here, you take it," Vic said smilin'.

Vic picked up a chair and started swingin' it around, clubbin' ev'rything in sight. Dadge used the bar to hammer CDs to bits and finished destroyin' the machines. The two laughed like demons unleashin' their anger.

"Wait, I think I hear something," said Dadge.

"I don't hear nothin'. You're just scared. Keep breakin' stuff," said Vic. "I gotta take pictures."

"What'a you have to do that for?"

"If I don't have nothin' to show, it don't count."

"There it is again," said Dadge. "I know I heard somethin' that time."

Vic stopped takin' pictures and listened.

"I hear it, too," he said.

The boys almost knocked each other over hurryin' outside. They ran, hidin' further down the alley behind a fence. It was bells they heard. The sound of bells kept getting' louder.

"What is that?" asked Dadge.

"Duck down," said Vic.

A minute later they saw what it was.

"It's that crazy old man. The one with the rabies dog," Vic said.

The old man's cart jingled as he walked down the alley. No dog with him this time. He paused a moment, in front of the fence where the boys were hidin'. Then he went on his way. It was then they saw the tall man walk back to the buildin'. They saw the light flick on. When they heard the man yell sentences made up of only swear words, Vic set the bar down, and then they ran away as fast as they could.

Fifteen minutes later the two stood pantin' back next to Coen's.

"What do you think the old man was doin' there?" asked Dadge.

"How should I know?"

"I mean, what do you think he was doin' there just then?"

"I don't know, but if he hadn't come along when he did, we'd have gotten caught in there and gotten our asses beat."

"What was that all about anyway? Why did we break up all that stuff?" asked Dadge.

"Ant'ny had me wreck it 'cause that guy was running a CD scam in their territory."

"How do run a scam with CDs?" asked Dadge.

"That's where some guys run around sellin' CDs to suckers sayin' they're a hard-workin' group that needs a start."

"Isn't the group any good?"

"There *is* no group. They put any kind of music on there. Every time they sell one, they make five or ten bucks for nothin'!"

"That's a lot of money. Maybe we should do that."

"Don't be stupid. They mess guys like that up if they don't quit. That's a sure way to get exed out. You should see all the money and gold and shit that Ant'ny walks around with. He's got a roll of hundred-dollar bills."

"Hundreds? No way."

"I seen it. Pretty soon I'm gonna be walkin' around with a roll. Bigger than Ant'ny's, and more gold chains! Him and Raphael's gonna get me in."

"How much did you make tonight for messin' up that guy's stuff?"

"Well... I didn't make anything for that. I had to show Ant'ny I wasn't some punk. I'll start making real money now. You'll see!"

"Half of nothin' is nothin'. So that's what I get for almost getting my head bashed in? Maybe that guy had a knife or a gun and could've killed us!"

"Did you *see* a gun in there when we was tossin' it? Stop talkin' like a kid. You better grow up if you wanna hang with me. See you later."

Dadge walked home slow and alone from there. Plenty of time for him to think about what he'd done. More important, he had time to think whether he'd do somethin' like that again – or maybe somethin' worse. He was carryin' quite a burden for a ten-year-old. Dadge was startin' to grow up older than his years.

CHAPTER 4. HI STARTS TO LOOK LIKE SANTA. AUGUST

*A*bout ten days later the kids were standin' around outside of Coen's as usual. I was inside talkin' to Leah while she was makin' me a sandwich – a sandwich I was *payin'* for, of course. It was a cloudy day and cool for August, about seventy-five. Leah was almost ready with my lunch when we heard the jinglin' of all those bells. Max went outside to see the latest. There came Hi dressed crazy as ever. His hair was longer, and his beard had filled in white as cotton. This time he was wearin' an old straw hat – the kind somebody wears when they're workin' in the garden. Only this one looked like it had been thrown away. It was missin' some straw on one side of the wide brim.

The old man had stuck some colorful things into the straw to dress it up. Stuck in it was an action figure, a yellow sand shovel, a toy car, and a plastic dinosaur. All kinds of other colorful things made it look like a cuckoo's nest turned inside out. He had a green vest on over a red shirt, blue shorts, his regular red sneakers, and black socks.

He'd made up a leather collar for Dancer with jingle bells on it and had him hooked up to the front of his cart with a couple old leashes like a sled dog. The ringin' of the bells on his cart and the bells on the dog attracted a lot of attention. So did his colorful outfit and the toys on his hat. There must'a been twenty kids followin' him.

"Look at that man," I heard Max's scorn from where I was inside the store. "A regular Pied Piper with those kids."

"Are you going to feed all of those kids?" goaded Amir, the proud owner of the tobacco store next door. It had become a habit for the two of men to pass the time of day talkin' together where their stores met, at times when biz'ness got slow. The two were dif'rent from one another in ways you couldn't even count, not just their appearances. Amir bein' a lean, young man in his early thirties while Max was in his late sixties and big around. "How are you going to afford that?" Amir continued.

"We already feed four of them. My wife, Leah, she's the one giving them food. Me, I don't care."

"I wouldn't give them the tobacco from one of my cigarettes! They're beggars. Let them work night and day like we do, then they can buy what they need from the money they earn."

That's what they said - 'cept neither one of *them* was workin' just then.

"It's for her I do it. I let her give them some scraps. No more than that! Just scraps."

"Listen Max. I'm not the kind of man who tells another

man what to do. But if *I* were you, I'd say to my wife, 'A store is for selling. Giving away our things to a lot of people, just because they put their hands out is too much! If you want to give our things away for nothing, go! Go find another husband who wants to work just as hard and who wants to give his things away like you do.' That's what I'd say. Of course, I wouldn't say that to *my* wife."

"You're right, Amir. Too long I've let this go on. First, it's one stranger, then it's two, then it's three. I should feed the whole world and let myself go hungry? No more! Today is the last day. I'm going in there after the lunch trade is done and put my foot down. You'll see!"

"There's that crazy old man again," I heard Vic declare to the three other kids. "I wish he'd drop dead!"

"Don't say that," said Sam. "I like him."

"So do I," said Pauly. "He's got toys!" he yelled, hoistin' his hands over his head. Half-a bear got flung up with his hands when he said that, the over-loved bear lookin' like a flag that had been through the losin' side of a war.

"What do you mean 'he's got toys' Pauly?" asked Dadge. "What kind of toys?"

"The kids say he finds toys in the garbage and fixes them up," said Pauly.

"What does he do with them all?" asked Sam.

"Maybe he gives them away, because he's nice," said Pauly.

"I haven't heard anyone say he gave them anything," said Dadge. "Maybe he sells 'em."

"Maybe he *can't* fix 'em," said Vic. "Maybe he's a garbage man who collects garbage."

"Let's go see," said Sam.

The kids ran up to the cart, puttin' their hands all around the top of it lookin' down in. Hi didn't mind the curiosity one bit. The more kids were around him, the happier he got.

"Look, a skateboard! That's what I want," said Dadge, grabbin' it off the top of the pile without askin'.

"That's junk," said Vic. "It only has three sets of wheels. Some dope's probably already broken his neck on it. You don't want that or you're stupid. It's nothin' but garbage!"

"Can you really fix this Mr. Engle?" asked Dadge as he turned the thing around lookin' it over.

"It will take some doing, but I sure can. I'll have to find another skateboard for the wheels."

"You're a liar!" Vic yelled. "The top is cracked. This thing's nothin' but junk. Just like the rest of the garbage you got."

"The top *is* cracked," said Dadge.

Dadge hung his head and put the broken skateboard back into the cart.

"Nobody can fix that," Dadge said, and turned his back on Hi, and walked away.

"Come on Dadge," said Vic. "Wishin's for kids. We'll take what *we* want."

By this time, I had my sandwich. My curiosity got the better of me, so I went over to have a look into Hi's cart for myself. Dadge and Vic had walked away, and some of the other kids who'd been watchin' had also walked away by then. I can't say as I blame 'em after seein' what was in the cart. I couldn't see what good could come from any of it.

"We're meetin' Raphael at ten tonight. He's takin' us to meet the head guy," I overheard Vic say. "I'll come by your place at nine-thirty."

"I don't think that's good…"

"You be ready then or you're out!"

"Alright, Vic. I'll see you later."

Pauly and Sam were stuck like glue on Hi and his cart full'a broken stuff.

"I want a baseball glove," said Pauly.

"You can't catch, and you know it," said Sam.

"If I had a glove I could catch. It's big so I wouldn't miss so much."

"That's true," said Sam. "Do you have a glove, Mr. Engel?"

"I don't have one yet. But when I find one, it will have your name on it, Pauly. And is there something you want, Sam?"

"No. I don't need anything from in there. Come on, Pauly. Let's go."

"There must be something you want," Hi said as they were leavin'.

"Nothing *you* can give me," Sam said quiet, lookin' down.

Sam led Pauly away. There's nothin' worse than offerin' false hope to the hopeless, and Sam knew that.

"What's he mean? Is he gonna give me a glove with my name on it?"

"No. There's no such thing. Mr. Engel means that he'll give it to you, like a *present* that has your name on it."

· · ·

I didn't spend much time with the kids back then. I liked 'em alright, but it made me sad to be around 'em. I knew how hard life was gonna be the older they got, and I didn't want to get too close when things started gettin' worse. Vic was already headin' into crime with Dadge likely to follow. They'd prob'ly end up in prison if they lived long enough. Poor Sam would end up workin' for the same man her mother's workin' for. And Pauly, well... he wasn't gonna stay innocent for more than a year or two more. That's the way I saw things back then.

It was later that day, after the lunch business trailed off, that Max talked to Leah in the back room while the help kept on slicin' meat behind the counter.

"Mama, this is the last day you feed those kids!"

"What do you mean? Where did this come from? I've been feeding them since last winter. So why should I change now?

"We can't give the store away. I've told you before. What if we sold cars? Should we give them each an automobile?"

"Max, a few slices of meat and some bread, we'll never miss it."

"It's too much! Some of my own relatives I wouldn't feed for free."

"Max, you know I love you. Well, I also love the children."

"After today no more! They only come here every day because you feed them. They have families and homes of their own. Let their own people take care of them."

"Max, this is not about sandwiches. Don't you look in their eyes? They need love. Pastrami and some chicken salad they could live without. I know they have people. Can't you see the way they stay together all day long? They've made each other their family because their people don't care about them. What if our Sarah had no one to love her? Shouldn't you want someone to care about her?"

"Feeding those kids can't bring our Sarah back. Let the past be buried in the past. Leave our Sarah out of this."

"Max, when we got married, we loved each other as much as two young people could. Ever since we lost Sarah, you've been different. You shouldn't give out love in such thin slices. It's not good for your heart. A heart should be like a well. As soon as you take out a glass full of water, the well is full again. Try to give some love away. It will be good for you. Please, Max. I want you to be the man I married so many years ago."

Max looked down at the floor. He loved Leah too much to say no to her. But he took some time for his pride's sake before givin' his reply.

"Alright. One more week! We'll feed them for one more week and no more. After that, no more free food!"

"Thank you, Max, I love you, too. And after next week, we'll make it the next week also."

CHAPTER 5. DADGE AND VIC MEET JUBBA. END OF AUGUST

*I*t was past nine-thirty when Vic went to Dadge's to get him.

Vic yelled loud and knocked on the apartment door, "You home, Dadge?"

The door opened, but it wasn't Dadge. It was his brother, who was older, taller, and a lot stronger than Vic.

"What'a you want?" he said real loud.

"Dadge in? We got someplace to go."

"Come on in," he said grabbin' Vic by the front of his shirt. He yanked him in so hard, Vic whipped around, fallin' to the floor. "And stay down!"

"What's wrong with you, man?" Vic said lookin' up.

"Hey Dadge, your girlfriend's here!" said the brother.

"What's wrong with you?" Vic yelled, rubbin' the back of his head where it got slammed.

When Dadge felt Vic hit the floor and heard his brother holler, he ran out of his room ready for trouble.

"What are you doin'?" Dadge said. "What do you have to go hittin' him for?"

"I didn't hit him, he fell, 'cause he's weak like you. If I want'a hit somebody I'll hit 'em. I don't need your permission!"

Then he hauled off and punched Dadge with a right cross makin' his head spin some.

"I can beat you up any day, stupid!" said Dadge's brother.

Vic jumped up ready for a brawl, but Dadge stepped in between him and his brother quick, like a ref holdin' two boxers apart. They were both swingin' at each another with Dadge getting' the worst of it in the middle.

"Don't hit him, Vic."

"I'll beat the shit out of him. Who's he think he's pushin' around?"

"Don't hit him. Let it go."

Dadge gave Vic a couple more shoves, hard enough to keep him away from his brother. Not too hard to get Vic any madder.

"C'mon Vic, don't bother with him. He's not worth it. He's always fightin'."

"You're an asshole!" Vic yelled at Dadge's brother.

"You can't take it!" the older boy said, jabbin' at him with his words to get him to fight some more. "You won't fight 'cause you know I can whip you!"

"C'mon, Vic. I'm telling you, don't mess with him."

Vic finally headed for the door and made it through with Dadge's brother callin' him things like "coward" and "weak." Vic sure wanted to beat the hell of him. In the end, he left takin' the insults.

"I know you wanted to mess with him," Dadge said out in the hall, "but once he starts hittin', he doesn't stop."

"Why's he gotta be like that? Where your folks at? Don't they do nothin'?"

"He's not like that when they're around."

" 'Cause your old man gives him a whippin'?"

"No way. Where do you think he learned it from?"

"Good thing he stopped messin' with me," said Vic braggin' "We got someplace to go. Wait 'till you meet Raphael. He's as cool as they come."

Ten o'clock rolled around. The city with all its lights kept things so bright, it was hard to tell it was dark out. No place for 'em to hide in the shadows where they were waitin'. They didn't feel like they were doin' wrong anyway. At least Vic and Raphael didn't. Dadge was a dif'rent story. He hadn't made his mind up yet which side of the fence he was gonna live his life on. This edgy stuff was all new to him.

"Raphael's lettin' us in, so you have to be cool when you meet The Man," said Vic.

"What should I do?" asked Dadge.

"You don't do nothin'. You say 'yes, sir' when he asks you somethin'."

"I don't call anybody 'sir'. What do I have to say that for?"

"You say that 'cause he's somebody. That's why. Raphael's bringin' us over so the guy can check us out. Here he comes. What's up, Raphael?"

"Hey," he said, holdin' out his fist to tap theirs. "What happened to you guys," he said, lookin' at their bruises.

"It's nothin'," said Vic. "We had to take care of somethin', that's all."

"You two ready to move up the ladder? Tonight you gonna meet The Man himself, Jubba."

"Jubba? You mean he's some fat guy?" asked Dadge.

"He's a fat dude *and* a fat cat," said Raphael.

Raphael pulled a knife from his back pocket and held it up in front of Dadge's eyes. "Only don't call him Jubba to his face or he'll cut you!"

"When did you get that?" Vic asked, holdin' out his hand.

"This is nothin'," said Raphael, droppin' the knife into Vic's hand. "Pretty soon I get a piece."

"A gun?" Dadge asked. "Where are you gonna get a gun?"

"All of Jubba's men get guns. That's why nobody messes with him."

"How do you rate one?" asked Vic. "You must have to steal somethin' expensive."

"First Jubba has you steal a few cars. Then you have to beat the crap out of some guys. You keep workin' up like that."

"So, what's this guy's real name. Is it Jubba, or somethin' else?"

"That's the only name *I* know him by. Jubba is what he likes to be called on the street. We can talk about him like this, but don't you let him hear you. Only thing he likes better than to be called Jubba on the street, is to mess up anybody he catches callin' him that. You say 'yes, sir, no, sir' to him. Got it!" Raphael said jabbin' his finger into Dadge's chest.

Vic took one last look at the chrome blade. He bounced the

knife in his hand a couple of times to feel the balance, before handin' it back.

"Shouldn't we go soon?" Dadge asked. "Where're we goin' anyway?"

"I don't know where we're goin'," said Raphael. "Nobody knows where Jubba's place is until they ex somebody out. They're comin' to pick us up. They're gonna want to see how tough you guys are. If they hit you, don't hit 'em back, or they'll give you twice as much. That's the deal."

A black, low-ridin' Cadillac ESV pulled up while they were talkin'. They couldn't see who was inside through the tinted glass. Two tough-lookin' body builder types got out, one from the front seat one from the back. Raphael took charge of Vic by punchin' him in the stomach. Vic didn't dare punch Raphael back. He just took it. Then, Raphael gave him a hard punch in the nose and pushed him inside the car. Dadge started to get in when one of the tough guys pulled him right out again. The guy punched Dadge in the gut.

"*Now* you get in," the guy said.

Dadge went to get in again when the guy pushed. Dadge hit the side of his head, on the top of the door frame. He winced and got in, followed by Raphael. One guy went back to sittin' shotgun in the front seat. The other guy climbed in the back, closin' the door behind him.

"Man, we're sure gettin' it good tonight," Vic said low to Dadge.

It had a limo seat facin' backwards, so the three of 'em, Vic, Dadge, and Raphael sat shoulder to shoulder facin' the back of the car. They were lookin' around at the fancy interior. There was a big screen TV above their heads. In front: a table, bar, and a computer screen. The tough guy sat facin' 'em in one of the two chairs that looked forward.

"Hand over your phones. Put these on and shut up!" the guy said, handin' 'em black eye masks. The guy checked to make sure the masks were on right so none of 'em could see anything.

They couldn't see, but they could hear the tough guy in the front seat talkin' to the driver about some job they were goin' to pull. Then, the radio got turned up loud to drown it all out.

They were there to move up in the world. They weren't thinkin' about blowin' the deal. They knew better than to fight back or have a look around without their mask on. One wrong move could make 'em look like they didn't belong. It was time to act cool, so the three of 'em sat still tryin' to figure out where they might be headed. That car didn't let any street sounds in, and it was impossible for 'em to figure where they were from the bumps in the road. So, they sat there waitin' and thinkin' what would happen next.

The twenty-minute ride seemed to go on forever. They weren't sweatin' it. They *wanted* to go meet the head man. Finally, the car stopped.

"Don't touch your masks," the tough guy said.

He jostled all their masks to be sure they still couldn't see anything. The car engine and music shut off and the two guys from up front got out. They heard the doors next to 'em open and Vic and Dadge felt strong hands around the tops of their arms as they were pulled out onto the sidewalk. After that, Raphael heard 'come on', as the tough guy from the back made *him* get out too.

Each tough guy, includin' the driver, took hold of the arm

of one rookie. They were pushed up into a buildin'. Raphael was the first one to get shoved up the stairs after that. He fell, not knowin' the stairs were there. The tough guys showed no mercy, pushin' and pullin' each of 'em. They took it easier on Raphael than the newbies. Vic and Dadge fell a few times. After makin' it up a flight of stairs and down a hallway, the three were made to stand next to each other.

"Okay," they heard, "you can take the masks off now."

They were in a good-sized room. The place was nothin' but a run-down dump. The dozen or so men that were around the room weren't holdin' any weapons, but they didn't hide the fact that they were all packin'. The three stood still, afraid they'd say or do somethin' wrong. There in front of 'em, was the man himself, Jubba. He sat in a huge leather chair wearin' a maroon suit, a leopard-skin hat, and dark sunglasses, and he left his shirt open to show off all his gold chains. He had gold rings with diamonds that glittered on all his fingers. The chair creaked and the leather squeaked ev'ry time he moved the slightest bit. He sat there lookin' 'em over. He lit a cigar, puffed on it a few times, and blew the smoke in their direction. Nobody said a word or moved, only Jubba smokin'. After Jubba mashed out the butt, he motioned with his chin, never sayin' a word.

Two of his men from the car were on either side of the boys with the third in back of Dadge.

"C'mon," one of 'em said, so the boys followed. Jubba smiled and motioned. Most of his men went out of the room followin' the boys. The men and the boys all went through a door into a back room. The man in charge of Dadge put his hand on Dadge's shoulder, stoppin' him just inside the door. The other men made a circle around Raphael and Vic.

"Okay, now fight your way out of the circle," one of the keepers said.

The men started laughin' as they beat the two boys, pushin' 'em around. It sure was a mean game. Dadge looked up at his guard. The man replied to his silent question; "You get it like that next time – *if* you come back."

The boys got punched bad all over, includin' in the face. When one of 'em fell, a man with a stick came over and beat 'em, showin' no mercy 'til they got up. The men had a high old time beatin' the boys, and they kept gettin' beaten, 'til the men thought they had enough.

"Okay. You're two are tough alright," said one of the men.

With that, the blindfolds were handed back to 'em, and they stumbled downstairs. They went out of the buildin' and then pushed down into the car for the return trip.

In the car, Dadge was the most shook up. Maybe 'cause he was the youngest, or maybe 'cause it was hard to watch what could'a happened to him. Vic and Raphael were bleedin' some, from their lips and noses, so the keeper threw a towel from the bar at each of 'em.

"Don't bleed on the car."

The boys didn't say a word. Just held the towels up to their faces tryin' to be men. After a good, long while the car stopped.

"Take off them masks," the keeper commanded. "Get out."

The keeper took back the masks and towels and all three boys got out. The car sped off, leavin' the three in the dark.

"This ain't where they picked us up," said Vic.

"This is part of it," said Raphael. "They left us in a bad part of town. We gotta figure out how to get back from here."

Raphael took a look around and said: "I think I know where we are. Let's go this way," he said pointin' in a direction.

"Why'd we go through all that beatin' and didn't get to hang with Jubba?" asked Vic.

"Yeah. And how come they beat you and not me?" asked Dadge as the three walked on.

"That was my second beating. First time I lost this tooth here," Raphael said raisin' his lip to show the gap. "This was light stuff. You get real beat up when they jump you in. They'll *all* have sticks then. I seen it done to a couple guys. They let me watch that, like they let *you* watch this time. If you're chicken, you don't come back for more. They have to know you're gonna be there when things get thick that's why they do it like this."

"Did you see how tripped out that car was?" Raphael said braggin' as if he owned it. It was his way of hidin' how much he was hurtin. "I bet that set Jubba back a hundred grand. I'm gonna get a car like that someday. You'll see! Then *I'll* be drivin'!"

"That car was amazin'. I never saw anything like *that* before. The inside looked like some fancy hotel room or something," said Vic. "How come that car was so much, but the place they took us to was so bad? Why wasn't Jubba's house tripped out like that?"

"That's not Jubba's house. He don't have a house," said Raphael. "He moves around so nobody can ex him. One day he'll be in one dive and the next day in another. That's how he stays alive!"

"He must have a house. Where does he keep all his food!" Vic said to make the others laugh. "He sure is one fat mother! I never seen somebody so fat, 'cept on TV."

"I never saw so many guns," said Dadge. "Everybody had guns. Some of the guys let their jackets fly open on purpose to show 'em off. They all had guns except us."

"I *told* you," said Raphael. "You get a gun after you're in. I'm gonna have a limo, a gun, more gold chains than Jubba, and about ten women. You'll see!"

The stars were shinin' bright that night, but the boys didn't notice. That's what happens when you head down a bad road. There are never any stars in that world, 'cause you're too busy lookin' around corners to notice 'em.

CHAPTER 6. HI'S CART SCAM. MIDDLE OF SEPTEMBER

*I*t was the middle of September, and summer was over. Leah knew Sam was cuttin' school 'cause she came by for a visit durin' school hours one day. So, Leah thought it was time for a talk.

"Come in, my bubala. You can watch while I make your sandwich," Leah said, welcoming her. "Come, come into the back room. It won't take a minute. Do you want maybe some coleslaw with that?"

"No thank you, Mrs. C. The sandwich will be enough."

"You're so thin. You should eat. Go in the back room and sit, while I slice the meat; nice and thick the way you like it."

"I've never been back here before."

Sam walked slowly between the refrigerated glass display cases that held all the meats sittin' in rows on shelves. She walked past the slicer where Leah was busy cuttin' turkey for the sandwich. She waited a minute before she reached her

hands out like she was divin'. She divided the curtains in half
and entered the back room for the first time. It was simple and
more dark than light. A bare lightbulb hung from wires over
the old enamel table. Sam pulled the cord and flicked the light
on. She looked around. She felt like she was in a special place.

There was a refrigerator next to the table. Sam opened it. It
was filled with stuff you'd have in a house, like mayonnaise,
milk, lettuce, and things. The wall next to the table had some
photos hangin' on it. There was one of a man and woman
standin' in front of a store. Sam recognized the buildin' and
the people alright, but there was no sign up, and there was
plywood nailed over where the window ought'a be. The glossy
photo was cracked and looked shrunk-up old. Sam took that
one off the wall to look at it close. It said June 7th, 1975 on
back in pencil.

Leah walked in puttin' the turkey on the table along with
some bread. Then she went in the refrigerator and took out
everything else they needed for lunch and sat down across
from Sam. Sam kept starin' at that picture. She knew it was
Mr. and Mrs. C., but they looked so dif'rent.

"Then, this is you and Mr. Coen?" Sam asked, holdin' up
the picture to show Leah, who was now old enough to be her
grandmother.

"Yes! This is me, and this is my Max. He was so handsome.
At least I thought so. Mostly he was very nice," she said as she
fixed their sandwiches.

"And this is the store too – isn't it?" Sam asked, flippin' the
picture over to show Leah the writing on the back.

Sam liked the feelin' she got in that room. She didn't know
Leah's flowered dress was out of date. The flowers, soft cotton

cloth, and her warm smile made the round woman seem like someone's mom. Sam sat across from her like she was hypnotized, watchin' her fix lunch.

"Yes, 1975. That's the year we bought the building. Max, he was so proud. He never went to college. It was because of his father he wanted to own his own store. You see, his father was a butcher who always had to work for someone else. Max wanted to be a businessman. So, he worked and worked day and night until he had enough money to buy the building!"

Sam kept lookin' around. Most of the room had shelves with goods ready to go up on the grocery store shelves. Across from the table was a bureau with a framed photo of a girl, a little older than Sam. There was also a burnt down white candle next to the photo and a menorah with candles.

"Who's that girl?" Sam asked, pointin' to the picture.

"That's our Sarah when she was ten."

"I didn't know you had a daughter. Where is she?"

"She's in heaven with the other angels, darling. She was never strong. Here's a picture of her when she was just a baby," said Leah, leanin' over and takin' another picture off the wall. It was another old photo of Leah and Max, but his time they were holdin' a baby. "She was such a good baby. She only cried when she needed something." Leah stared at the picture like she was havin' a hard time lettin' go. "She was such a happy baby." She took a deep breath and let out a sigh. Then, real careful, she put the picture back on the wall. "And how old are you?"

"I'm eight, but my birthday's in March, so I'm almost nine. She's very pretty."

"We lost our Sarah two months after this picture was

taken. She was so smart, and such a good girl, like you. So polite."

Sam blushed and hung her head while she started to eat. Leah quickly wiped away a tear with her napkin.

"So, tell me, Sam, why aren't you in school today? I don't think this is the first day you've missed either, is it? And the school year has just begun."

"I take Pauly to school every morning, then I don't go."

"Oh, I see," she said in such a way Sam would know she wasn't disappointed in her. "So why don't you go inside?"

"Vic doesn't go to school. And Dadge doesn't go much either. I don't see why I gotta go if they don't have to."

"You *should* go. Listen. You can do a lot with your life. You're too young to give up. You're smart, this I know. Don't worry about what Vic does. He's heading for trouble – so I've heard. I'll tell you what. If I can get Dadge to go to school every day, will promise me you'll go too?"

"Okay. I guess."

"Good! In the meantime, you go to school. I'll talk to Dadge, and before you know it, you'll both be going to school regular again!"

That's the way Sam told me it went, 'cept Sam said she made like she sneezed to use her napkin to wipe her own eyes after hearin' about Sarah. I've noticed it's when we're sittin' across from one another eatin', that dif'rences seem to fade away. It's when you're talkin' from the heart that you only notice familiarities. Leah got to play mama for a while, and Sam got to play daughter. Only, they were more than just playin', they were both wishin' it, too.

That's how Sam spent her lunchtime inside that day. I ate

my lunch a little early 'cause I went on a hunt *outside*. I hadn't seen Hi around for some time, so I went lookin' for him. I decided to stalk after him to see how he was spendin' his days. So, I walked across town to his apartment buildin'. Sure enough, Hi was sittin' on the front stoop. He wasn't lookin' real well. His beard had grown in and was gettin' some length to it. His hair was long, too, as long as Will Shakespeare's. He had long pants on, which was an improvement over shorts. He was wearin' his ridiculous red sneakers, as he us'ally did, checked tan pants, and a green and red plaid shirt. When I say he didn't look good, I mean the man, apart from the way he dressed. Looked like he had some bruises on his face.

"Hello Poet. What brings you by?"

The question brought Dancer to life. The mutt started barkin' its head off. He came right up to me and started lickin' my hand. I was standoffish. I don't like dogs much, and I didn't want to get that friendly with Hi.

"You did. I came by to see if you're okay. I haven't seen you in more than a week. You feelin' alright, Hi?"

"My cart is broken. One wheel went flat. Look, I'll show you."

Hi got up from the stoop and went around the side of the buildin' and he was limpin'. He dragged the cart out from around there and it was all banged up. One wheel was flat like he said, and the wire cage was bent up some too.

"What in the world happened?"

"I fell. My cart was loaded with so many fine things for the children, I wasn't paying attention where I was going. I went off a curb and fell. The cart dumped out and I lost everything!"

"You fell? Or were you pushed? You're limpin' pretty bad."

"I, I, I fell," he stuttered. "There's no way anybody could attack me with Dancer around."

"I guess you're right about that. Dancer could just about lick anybody to death."

"If you could help me," he said, without missin' a beat, "I have a spare cart in my apartment. If you could get my cart upstairs, I could use one of the wheels from the other cart. Do you think you could do that for me?"

"Well, at least it's not a hundred and ten degrees out. But I don't know about climbin' all those steps."

"Please, Poet. I have a lot to do before Christmas. There are so many presents to get ready. I can't let the children down."

I've known a lot of delusional people in my time. I'll spend time with delusional people and even folks that are just plain crazy. I don't care, so long as they're good folks. I still didn't know which side of the fence Hi was on. I wasn't sure if he was on the good side or not. But I gave in 'cause he looked so pathetic.

"I guess it's alright this one time. Come on. You help me drag that thing upstairs, and I'll give it a go."

That staircase wound up and around the inside of that buildin' like the stripe on a barber pole. I had to go up and around seven times to climb to his floor. There wasn't any weight to the cart, seein' how it was empty. It was just a pain in the ass doin' labor for somebody who was wastin' his time collectin' junk. Dancer followed waggin' his tail and droolin'. At least he wasn't barkin' anymore. But I did have to watch to be sure he didn't get underfoot and trip me up. We finally made it all the way to the seventh floor, and I was mighty tired. I wasn't used to doin' any kind'a work anymore anyway.

Hi put his key in the lock and opened the old dark-wood door. On the inside, the door frame had just enough wood for the latch to catch onto. It had been busted out so many times from people kickin' the door in through the years.

"Here we are!" he declared as if we had reached his palace. "Please come in. Can I get you a cold glass of water?"

"I'd rather take whiskey. Do you have some to spare?"

"I don't keep any in the house. I don't drink."

"Water it is then."

I pulled the damaged cart into his livin' room and took a good look around while Hi was in the kitchen. His place sure was a disaster. He had things stacked on the floor and piled on the furniture. There were a lot of broken things for kids and some toys so old, no kid today would pay attention to. And I never saw so many Christmas decorations. Box upon box of decorations. Old decorations made of glass with most of the silver givin' up. Garland, enough to go around the block a few times, and lights of all dif'rent kinds, not hardly one string matchin' another. Dancer followed me around. Ev'ry time I reached down to open a box from curiosity, Dancer mashed his wet nose against my hands.

"Here's your water. Thank you again for helping me."

"No problem," I said. I took a sip or two to take some time, as to not spring questions on him right away. I waited a short while, then I started in.

"You sure got a lot of stuff here. I've never seen so many Christmas decorations 'cept in stores. I didn't think they even made tinsel anymore. And you got boxes and boxes of it. Where'd it all come from?"

"I have a job working in a thrift store three blocks down. I get twenty percent off employee discount."

"Hi, can I ask you somethin'?" I waited for him to say somethin' but he didn't. He just stared back at me with his piercin' blue eyes wide open, and that peaceful smile. He was lookin' more than a little crazy. "Hi, you don't really think you're Santa Claus, do you?"

"I never said I was. I love Christmas. It's the most wonderful day of the year. God made the day for children's wishes and dreams to come true."

"You weren't around when I was a kid 'cause my Christmases weren't exactly what you'd call a dream. I got shuffled around from one home to the next so many times, if I ever *did* get somethin' I wanted for Christmas, I'd be lucky if they wrote the right name on the tag."

"I know not all children get what they want. There have to be adults who help to make their dreams come true. That's what I'm doing. I'm one of the people who help make children's most important wishes come true."

"You know, there are lots of poor families who'd be mighty insulted, you givin' things to their kids."

"Ohhh! These toys aren't for poor children," he said like he was shocked. "These are for children who have no one to care about them. They're the ones *I'm* here to help. The neglected children."

"Hi, honest enough, I don't see a toy here that's fit for a kid of today. If these things aren't too old, then they're too broken for kids to play with," I said as kind as I could. It was like he ignored the truth I was sayin' and he went on as if I never said it.

"There's something here for children for blocks around – even for the whole city! I have to start repairing some of the broken things and many of the toys only need painting."

Hi went into the other room and started rummagin' around. I'd taken a seat on the arm of the sofa. There was too much stuff to clear off any seat, so that was the only place to sit down. Dancer followed Hi and watched him like he understood what Hi was up to.

"There's so much to do," he said loud from the other room. "It's hard for me to find time now that I'm working in the store. Come December, I'm quitting the store, and I'll go to work full-time on these gifts."

After hearin' some boxes fall over and some metal clangin', Hi came back into the room draggin' and even sadder lookin' cart.

"Here's the spare cart I was telling you about, Poet. Tomorrow, I'll ask them at work if I can borrow some tools. The wheels on this cart will fit on my regular cart. Do you think you can come over tomorrow after I get home? I could use some help."

"No, Hi. I'm sorry. I don't want any part of what you're doin'. I know you mean well, but you're only goin' to disappoint a lot of kids. You got Dadge thinkin' he's goin' to get a skateboard. You keep tellin' him you're gonna fix one up for him. Pauly's lookin' forward to getting' a baseball glove. I don't see one here. An' you keep askin' Sam what she wants. These kids think you're gonna come through for 'em. Not to mention, I don't know how many other kids you've made promises to. I admit I'm gettin' very fond of those kids. I don't want to see the hurt in 'em the day after Christmas."

"I would never do anything to hurt children. I believe, when children are at their best, you can see God in them. They can be the most generous among us, willing to give love without measure. They can express hope and joy in a world that's all too jaded. They need help. *Our* help. And that's what I do for them every Christmas."

"You mean you've done this before?"

"Every Christmas for as long as I can remember. It's up to adults to do all we can, so children can be happy. I've come to this city to keep the spirit of generosity healthy and strong!"

"Those are fine words, Hi, but you're bitin' off more than you can chew. What you're tryin' to do is impossible. I'm afraid you're gonna make a mess of things."

"You'll see. I'll do it! Just you wait and see."

That was the second time I gave the poor guy a ballin' out. I was steamin' mad. Maybe Hi *was* a good person. That wasn't the point. It was gettin' the hopes of those kids up that got me. I stomped down the seven flights of stairs 'til I thought I'd punished the bottoms of my feet enough. Then I knocked on Jake's door, 1A.

Jake answered after a while. He had changed his wardrobe from the last time I visited the king of the castle. This time, he had on the same kind'a tee shirt, but with dif'rent stains.

"Hey Poet."

"Don't mean to bother you, but have you had any trouble with the guy I sent over? You know, the guy on the seventh floor who thinks he's Santa Claus."

"He pays his rent on time. That's all I care about."

"I just came down from there. He made me so mad. I was just wonderin'."

"Did he tear up the joint? I never go up that high."

"No. I'm sure the place doesn't look any worse than when you rented it to him 'cept he's turned it into a junk shop. He's got more Christmas decorations than a department store."

"What'd you go up there for? He a friend of yours?"

"I can't say we're friends. I was tryin' to help the guy out. His cart needed fixin'."

"Don't tell me he got you to drag that broken old cart of his up seven flights of stairs," he said laughin'. Then he kept on laughin'.

"How did you know? And what's so funny about that anyway? I was just tryin' to help out the old goat."

"Because you and a hundred other suckers have dragged that old cart up them steps," he said laughin' like a nut. "He must have conned the whole city by now. He's had three or four people drag that cart up those stairs every day for the past couple of weeks. Once in the mornin', once at lunchtime, and again after he gets back from work. Sometimes he fits two trips in at lunchtime. I bet you ten bucks he'll have it downstairs again as soon as you leave."

"Why would the man do somethin' like that? Have somebody drag that thing all the way upstairs just so he can bring it down again? Only one thing to call someone who goes on a fool's errand. I'll be a damned fool! Besides bein' crazy, I mean. I was crazy to think I could help a crazy man. And who are all these folks who come here to help him carry that thing? How could an old man like that, who's only been in town for a couple months, know that many people?"

"He makes friends easy, I guess. Some people are like that. Me, I'd rather stay alone in my own apartment and relax."

I was in a huff after talkin' to Jake. I left that place angry and confused.

CHAPTER 7. HI'S CART SCAM UNVEILED. MIDDLE OF SEPTEMBER

I didn't sleep right all night thinkin' about what Jake told me. So, the next day, I decided to go over to Jake's apartment buildin' to see what Hi was up to. I believed Jake was tellin' the truth, but I had a hard time believin' that Hi had gotten to know so many people. I made a good bit of my cash at the end of the day; pan-handlin' commuters between four and six. Ev'nin's when I had my regulars who bought a little somethin' from me.

Soon as I got up, I went over there. I got to Jake's about ten that mornin' and snuck around to make sure Hi wasn't goin' to catch me at spyin'. When I got there he was sittin' on the front stoop again, just like he was when I was there the day before. Dancer was lyin' next to him bein' petted. Hi had his old cart with the flat wheel hid around the side of the buildin'. He must'a dragged it down again just like Jake said.

It wasn't quite a half-hour later, a nice lookin' young couple come along and started talkin' to him. They said hello to Hi like they were old friends. Damn, that made me angry. I was still hot from the day before for feelin' like a fool, and now this!

"What happened to you, Hi?" the woman asked real nice like she was his own lovin' kin. "Did someone beat you up? That's a serious-looking black eye."

"We'll be glad to go to the police station with you if you want to file a report," the man said.

"Don't fuss over me. I'm just an old man who tries to do too much. I was wheeling my cart along the sidewalk yesterday, and I wasn't watching where I was going. I fell off the curb and broke my cart. Let me show you."

There he was havin' folks follow him around again. Dancer was by his side with the man and woman followin' him.

"Here's my cart. See? The wheel's caved in. I had an awfully hard time getting it home. I have a spare cart with a good set of wheels in my apartment. I could fix this one if I could get it upstairs."

Well, you can guess that he had the couple volunteer to drag the thing up seven flights of stairs. Only this time the thing was loaded down full of junk he had garbage picked.

"Be careful," he had the nerve to say when they weren't holdin' the cart up straight.

'Be careful of what? They gonna break your garbage,' I said to myself.

So, ev'rything Jake said turned out to be true. I wasn't done with Hi yet. I determined then and there to follow him around another day soon, to see how he knew all these folks. I left there madder than I was the day before.

CHAPTER 8. SAM'S MOTHER GRACE IS DRINKIN'. END OF SEPTEMBER

"**G**ive me another one."

She leaned heavy on the bar, slumped in her barstool, and started coughin' out of control but got out, "One more I said."

Sam's mother, Grace, always sat off to one side of the bar. She kept away from the middle 'cause there was a big mirror in the center of the back-bar. She didn't like seein' the reflection of the worn-out woman she'd become. Men had used up a little bit of her 'til now there wasn't much left.

"Do you think this stuff is good for you, Grace?" the bartender asked, pourin' her another shot and a half of cheap whiskey.

"It's not gonna hurt me, I can tell ya that," she said with half a smile toastin' him.

"Grace, it's none of my business, and I wouldn't say this if we wasn't friends, but you don't seem right lately. Don't you think you should take it easy?"

"I got a kid at home I have to take care of. I love her. I can't stand her to see me."

"What do you mean? If you love her, I mean. Why don't you want to see her?"

"No, I don't want *her* to see *me* like this," she said through her coughin'. That's what I'm sayin'. I had a regular job when I was carrying her. I knew her father wasn't gonna stick around. I didn't expect him to 'cause he wasn't the type." Grace took a gulp and took a deep breath after the coughin' stopped. "After she was born, I was alone with her. I didn't have nobody because my man was gone. So, I started workin' a little, off-hours. The regular job wasn't payin' enough for the kid and me, so I turned a trick now and then. I wasn't no street walker. It was somethin' I did on the side."

Grace leaned to one side to look at herself in the mirror. She saw a tired woman, worn painful thin. A poor soul, eaten up by the life that had chosen her.

"These were regular guys I knew. I felt bad about what I was doin'. You know, bein' a mother and doin' that. So, I took a little somethin' to take the edge off. You know, to make it easier. I used to think I'd get married and be in love. I never saw myself gettin' into this.

"Before I knew it, I was workin' for Jubba and shootin' up three, four times a day. Now my kid's alone most of the day and the money I make goes to Jubba or in my arm. I'm tryin' to cut back, but I get sick. I can't earn enough to pay for the stuff no more. I can't stand the kid seein' me like this. She looks up at me, and I can see she loves me. The look in her eyes just kills me!"

"It's not your fault, Grace. You're not the first person this has happened to. Don't beat yourself up about it. Why don't you have someone look after your kid and go someplace until you can get straightened out?"

"Because Jubba owns my ass, that's why. He'll cut me if I stop workin'. I asked him once and he slapped me down. He said he'd stop using me when I stopped breathin'."

"He's a bastard!"

"You're a good man, Mike. I should'a married somebody like you. Take care of yourself." Grace stood herself up and shuffled off, her eyes pasted on the door, careful not to look in the mirror on the way out.

CHAPTER 9. MAX AND AMIR DRINK COFFEE. BEGINNING OF OCTOBER

It was October and fall was takin' hold of things. The temper'ture was droppin' and the leaves were changin'. The city doesn't have a lot of trees. A park around here's only a patch, held next to the blanket of color stretched out on top of the rollin' hills of any countryside. But, the crunch of leaves underfoot and the smell of crisp air's prob'ly just about the same ev'rywhere you go. There can be a day when clouds are out makin' ev'rything feel moody gray. You turn a corner and there – bright yellows and reds surprise you! When trees put on color, it's like they're dressin' up just for ev'rybody to admire 'em. Ev'ry other season of the year, I can walk by a park, never thinkin' much about the grass or the trees. But when they stand around looking like their branches are holdin' up fireworks, I can't help but notice. Guess they're tryin' to tell us we're not supposed to take things for granted.

This year, fall brought on a change with Amir and Max, too. Seems like it was finally the season for those two old cats to change their colors. They'd known each other long past the time when they should'a been more familiar. They'd talk about ev'rything and anything most ev'ry day, so long as it wasn't anything important.

It was early afternoon that day when the two were talkin' together where their two stores met, as they often did. Through the years they had gotten used to one another. Max was a good landlord, and Amir was a good tenant. It took a long while, but they'd learned to trust each other. Besides that, they liked each other more than either would let on. The chill in the air was the nudge that finally made it happen.

"So Max, we talk so often. I've never said this before, but I think of you as a friend. I have fresh coffee. You haven't come in for a visit since I've been here. So why don't you come in? It's nice and warm inside."

"You have been a very good tenant. Never any trouble. And the rent is always there on the first of the month. Why shouldn't we be friends? After all, you've been in the store next door for ten years now."

"Twelve. It's been twelve years. April it will be thirteen."

"Alright, so it's twelve. Even better. We talk often. So now maybe some coffee together wouldn't hurt."

"I know it's not easy for you."

"Listen Amir, you're thirty years younger than I am."

"Almost forty Max."

"Alright, so we'll say thirty-five. I'm old, but I'm not backward. I'm very modern. I know times are changing every day."

"Why don't you come in and get away from business for a little while?"

"Business I don't mind. And I love my Leah! Ask anyone.

But still, a short vacation from her I could use," he said with a chuckle.

So, Max stepped foot into Amir's store. He walked around like he was in a foreign country. Like a regular tourist lookin' at ev'rything. He took a long look, admirin' the glass-enclosed walk-in humidor, which took up about a third of the store.

"This is my niece Kalila. You've met her before," Amir said as they walked past her to the back room.

"Yes, good to see you again. You get prettier every day."

"Thank you, Mr. Coen," she said smilin'.

"Kalila, watch the store for now," said Amir. "We'll be in the back room."

"I keep the front room plain," said Amir, "but back here I have many things from our country. I enjoy them. Please sit. I made this coffee only a half-hour ago. Have you ever had Arabic coffee?"

"No, I don't think so. Is it so different?"

"Maybe I should have asked first if you only eat kosher."

"It's fine. We're not so strict as we were years ago. Leah says, 'If God went through the trouble to create it, so why shouldn't we try it at least?'" he said with a smile. "I keep a kosher store because most of our customers are more strict than we are. If they knew how we felt maybe they would do business someplace else. They think to love God a person has to follow a book filled with rules. Leah and I don't think God is watching for us to make mistakes. We think he has better things to do."

"Sit, try some coffee. Like this: take a bite of the date and then a sip of coffee. So, you believe in God?"

"I know young people today, like you, think stories of God

are nothing but fairy tales. Leah and I used to be very devout. Then we lost our Sarah. You should have known Leah before. She was so happy. You'd think every day she was going to a dance. After that, both our hearts were broken. I was so mad at God for taking our daughter away. I didn't talk to him for a long time. Then one day I said to God: 'I know I can't understand why you do things the way you do. I also know in the end you'll be right, so I know better than to say anything against you. I hope you understand; I'm just a man. So for now, I'm going to stay angry with you until I understand better.' That's what I said to God. That was a long time ago. Sarah goes to temple sometimes. I don't go anymore. I'd feel like a hypocrite; to sit in Temple and be mad at God. That wouldn't be right. What about you, Amir? Do you talk to God?"

"I'm not agnostic. I'd like to believe there is a god. I can't say one way or the other. I don't know if there is a god or not. So, you haven't prayed since you lost your daughter?"

"I don't call it praying. That's too formal for someone I know so well. I used to say things to God so many times during the day, it was just talking. Now I talk to him once in a while. Mostly to complain," he said, taking a sip of coffee. "This is good! It's strong. It doesn't taste like coffee, but I like it."

"Thank you, Max. It takes some getting used to, and I think you'll like it even more once you give it a chance. I wonder about God. My wife and I haven't been able to have children. I think, if there was a god, he would have given us at least one child. Zara is such a good person."

"That's why Leah feeds those kids that come around. I

don't mind them so much, except that we shouldn't give the store away by feeding them – sometimes twice a day. I'm only glad we don't run a bank or maybe she'd be handing them money every day instead of sandwiches. She talks about them and has worries as if they were our own."

"Zara tries to treat her sister's children the same way. I try to tell her she shouldn't, but she won't listen. She needs to love children even if they aren't hers."

"Leah's the same way. She was the favorite aunt. The children in our family still think of her as special, but they're all grown. Now we have even a new generation. Leah loves them all, but now she knows it's never going to be the same as having our Sarah back."

"I don't know what to do about it. Someday, when Zara is past the time when she can have children, I'm afraid she'll make herself sick over it."

"So, Leah feeds a few of the children every day. No one cares about them, she tells me. It's not our job to love other people's children, I tell her. Now that old man with the dog, Hi. He's a pleasant enough person, I have nothing against him, but he thinks he's Santa Claus. He has all the children in the neighborhood believing they're going to get presents somehow. Now Leah's worried about *that*. 'What will happen if they don't get presents?' she asks me. Am I supposed to know? What's a man to do?"

"We'll continue to love them as they love us. That's all we *can* do."

"Of course. What else are we to do? Well, Amir, thank you for the coffee. Quite a fancy coffee pot you have. Very beautiful! I also like the middle-eastern decorations. Not so different from some things *we* have, except we only have rugs on our floors, not hanging on the walls," he said with a laugh. "And I've never had coffee like this either."

"I'm glad you enjoyed yourself. The coffee pot is always here. We'll talk again tomorrow. Let's have coffee again soon."

CHAPTER 10. MORE OF HI'S SCAMS AND PAULY LIVES WITH SAM. MIDDLE OF OCTOBER

*I*t was the middle of October and gettin' colder all the time. The cold is hard to take at my age. I'd put on extra layers to stand outside, and I cut my pan-handlin' down some. But worryin' about the cold in days past – *that* was the worst of it for me. I remember all the nights back then, when I had to make do outside, tryin' to sleep in the cold. I had my bases covered nowadays, moneywise, so I thought, but you can never know for sure.

Hi was gettin' more mysterious all the time. He'd stay disappeared for days at a time. Then suddenly, there he'd be again. I got up early one day and went to Jake's apartment buildin' to spy on Hi again. He stopped pullin' his trick about gettin' fools like me to pull his cart up to his apartment on the seventh floor. I didn't know what he was doin' these days, but I was determined to find out.

I had gone there nine o'clock a few days before only to find out he'd already left. Like lettin' a cat out of a bag; once it's out, there's no sense chasin' it. So, this time, I got to Jake's at seven-thirty. An ungodly hour for a man of leisure like myself to be up and around. Eight o'clock was the magic number. The front door opened like on one of those old-fashioned clocks, then the cuckoo came out with his dog. He sure looked like the worst imitation of Santa Claus I've ever seen. His real beard and long white hair didn't make up for his strange outfits.

He had on a red sweater over his white shirt. Over that he had on a green vest. Not a proper vest like a gentleman would wear. I mean, it was a vest; the kind you zip out of a winter coat. The bottom half of him was wearin' a pair of green plaid pants, and of course, his red sneakers. One good thing was, it had been too cold for him to be wearin' shorts, so at least his legs were covered up. He had gained weight, on purpose I'm guessin', so he could pretend even more to be like the jolly old elf himself.

He dragged his cart outside, down the stoop, and onto the sidewalk. It had more bells on it than ever, and they sure did jingle ev'ry time he moved it around. I noticed he didn't mind draggin' it this mornin', seein' as how it was mostly empty. Then he put a pair of those cloth, clip-on antlers on Dancer, and hitched him up to the front of it. Dancer had those round, jingle bells around his neck collar, and jingle bells on the harness that hooked him to the cart. He got goin', and he was really haulin'. I had a hard time keepin' up with those two and hidin', too. Why a man with nothin' to do all day was in such a hurry was somethin' I had to find out. He walked about ten blocks in the opposite direction of Coen's before somethin' happened.

As he was walkin' along, his wallet dropped out of his

pocket somehow. I saw the whole thing clear as day from the other side of the street where I had hid myself in an alley. I felt sorry for the old guy losin' his money, but I couldn't say anything or he would'a known I was followin' him around. There were a lot of folks walkin' to work by then. He kept on goin' and before he had gone much further, a young woman picked it up. She gave it a quick look and stuffed it into her coat without missin' a beat. She kept on walkin', so I knew she was gonna keep it.

I felt bad that I didn't do somethin' instead of just watchin'. I kept followin' him expectin' that he'd start havin' a real bad day first time he went to buy somethin'. But that's not how things went.

The next block, damned if he didn't drop another wallet! He did the same damn thing! Must'a done it accidentally on purpose the first time. Damn, I wished I had someone else with me, so folks would believe me when I told 'em later. I kept a keen eye on the wallet to see what was goin' to happen. I thought that maybe this was Hi's way of bein' Santa Claus, givin' money away like that. I figured he put five or ten bucks in the wallets, so folks who needed it would pick the wallets up. A woman, about mid-thirties, saw Hi drop it. She didn't even look inside. Could'a been a million dollars in there for all she cared. I crossed the street and crept up hidin' in a close-by alley to hear what was bein' said.

"Sir! Sir!" she hollered. "Sir, you dropped your wallet."

"Thank you, ma'am. That's very kind of you. Not everyone is as honest as you are. I don't know what I'd'a done. Poor Dancer and I might have missed a few meals if it weren't for you."

The lady looked so happy havin' been acknowledged for doin' a good deed like that. She bent down and gave Dancer a good pettin'. Dancer got up on his hind legs, jumpin' up and down makin' his bells ring. I wondered how the old man could'a taught the dog to do a trick like that without even givin' the dog a signal.

"I like your friend. Is he a dog or a reindeer?"

"He's a dog, of course, but he's a very special dog. Every Christmas Eve he becomes a real reindeer. He and I fly over the cities of the world giving presents to all the children no one else cares about. Look what I have in my cart."

The lady looked at him, like he was as crazy as I thought he was. He picked up a few things one at a time and told her how he was gonna fix 'em up to give to kids for Christmas. She couldn't help shakin' her head when he wasn't lookin' 'cause the things he showed her were plain, old nasty.

"All the unloved children for blocks around here are going to get what they wish for this Christmas. I'll see to that. I keep my promises. A little paint and a few nails, that's all I need! You should see what I do with these things."

"Really, that's such a wonderful thing you're doing," she said humorin' him. "You promised children?"

"Yes, ma'am. As many as ask. There are kids around here who wouldn't even get a thought on Christmas if it wasn't for me. You should come by to see all the beautiful toys I've saved up for them. Do you have children, ma'am? If you don't mind me asking."

"Yes, we have two. A boy and a girl."

"I live in the big brick apartment building on North Pine Street, one hundred, it's easy to remember. You and your husband should drop in next time you're in my neighborhood to see all the wonderful toys!"

"Yes, we'll be sure to do that," she said, musterin' up the biggest smile she could, considerin' what she was prob'ly thinkin'.

"I have to be off. Lots of toys to find and not many more days before Christmas!"

The lady stood starin' as Dancer pulled the cart away with Hi holdin' on. She shook her head one last time and walked away lookin' concerned. I didn't blame her. Then it dawned on me.

'Recruitin'! I said to myself. That's what he's doin'. The old con-man is recruitin'. God knows how many poor, unsuspectin' fools he got caught up in his web. Who knows how many he got hauled in already after all these days he's been around? Now, I knew. I knew how old Hi had got to know so many folks from all over the city.

I wasn't through with him yet. I wanted to keep followin' Hi to see how many wallets he'd drop as bait, but that was the end of his wallet droppin' for the day. Next, he walked about six more blocks 'til he made a ruckus outside a luncheonette.

He walked mostly into the place when a waitress told him, "You can't bring that dog in here, mister. You'll have to tie him up outside."

By the time he walked in with Dancer and turned his cart around, he had jingled ev'ry person's attention in the luncheonette to know he was there. He left the place and tied Dancer up to a sign post right out in front. Then, the old codger made like he was havin' a hard time untyin' Dancer from the cart. I had seen him hook up the dog to the cart back at Jake's apartment buildin', and it went easy as pie. Then he started askin' passerbys if they were any good at untyin' knots. He was at it again – recruitin'!

Of course, only the nicest folks would stop at all to listen. Finally, one man wearin' a long, brown coat stopped to help.

"I can't bring Dancer into the establishment. They don't allow dogs. And I can't leave him tied to the cart. That would block the sidewalk. My hands aren't as nimble as they used to be."

"That's alright, old-timer. I'm good at getting knots out. This won't take long."

Of course, he started in on his spiel again about the poor neglected kids and Christmas presents. After the man untied Dancer from the cart, Hi had no choice but to leave the dog there and go on in alone. He'd'a gotten caught if he tried tyin' the knot back in again. There were folks sittin' at tables by the front windows who had first-row seats like at a show. Dancer sat there quiet as could be the whole time.

After Hi went into the place, I got as close as I could to the door. I was hidin' in the next doorway, but still I wasn't close enough to hear or see what was goin' on. After a few minutes the door opened up and there was a loud commotion.

"Don't come back here again," I heard a mean soundin' man yell. "If you want food, you have to buy it. Don't come in here beggin' for scraps!"

"It's not for me, it's for my dog. He's very hungry."

Then I heard a bunch of folks holler back at the man sayin' things like: "don't yell at Santa", "he's only wantin' to feed his dog," and "what's the dif'rence if the food's goin' in the garbage anyway."

Then some folks came out the door with him and yelled back in: "You shouldn't throw Santa Claus out. He's a nice old man. He's not askin' for himself," and things like that.

Five people had followed Hi out onto the sidewalk. Now he had a regular congregation to convert.

"It's not for me I was asking. It's for my friend, Dancer. He was a starving stray only a short time ago. I don't want him to go without food. He remembers being hungry and I don't want to put him through that."

'Holy Hannah!' I thought. 'As if the dog is traumatized by eatin' a late breakfast.' I don't know how those people didn't all scatter to the four corners of the earth when they hear him layin' it on so thick.

"Here buddy," said one of the men, holdin' out a ten-dollar bill.

"Please, call me Hi. I couldn't take that much. I only need two dollars. Just enough for a can of dog food."

The man tried talkin' Hi into takin' the ten, but Hi wouldn't give in.

"No really. That's very generous of you, but it's not for me I'm asking. Two dollars, that's all I need."

"Well, I think I have a few singles," said a woman. She looked well-heeled, about mid-forties, and smiled as she went rummagin' through her bag.

"Here's a single," said a man about fifty, and handed it to Hi.

I was surprised to hear him refuse more money than just the two bucks he asked for. I thought maybe he was a confidence man. Turnin' down eight bucks now, to make the people think he was honest, and then, later on, he'd find a way to con 'em out of a hundred.

"I found a dollar," the high-brow lady said, holdin' it up like it was a prise.

Hi went right into his recruitin' speech about givin' Christmas presents away, and how he was gonna give each kid exactly what they wanted most for Christmas. And, of course, he told 'em exactly where he lived and how he had intentions to fix up all the broken junk he found.

I followed Hi all mornin' watchin' him con and recruit, con and recruit, over and over. He had all kinds of tricks. He dumped his cart over on purpose a couple times when he thought no one was watchin', and somebody would come along to help right the thing. He stood in front of a grocery store, holdin' out two bucks askin' strangers if they'd go in and buy food for Dancer, 'cause he didn't want to leave the dog tied up. Of course, only kind folks would go out of their way. It takes a special person to stop what they're doin' to go on a fool's errand for a stranger.

Next place Hi stopped in was a what-not thrift store. Only Hi didn't go to the front door like ev'rybody else. He went around back. By the time I snuck in close enough to spy on him, he had his cart almost full. I watched him dumpster dive the thrift store's garbage. He was loadin' up on broken, useless things the store couldn't sell or didn't want to try. Broken toys with missin' wheels, one-arm dolls, computer games that looked busted. I couldn't believe Hi actually had the time or the know-how to fix even one of 'em. 'Might as well give 'em all out to the bad kids to teach 'em all a lesson' – so I thought at the time.

Hi didn't miss a beat. He never sat still to watch the world go by. He didn't smoke, stop at the liquor store, or hang at bars. The man knew the way from one stop to another. He hit another thrift store dumpster a dozen blocks from the first one. There he filled his cart 'til it was over-flowin' with colorful, tarnished, and broken junk. I felt sorry for poor Dancer. He had to help pull the darn cart now that it was full.

Hi went over a few blocks and turned around, I guessed to go back home. I figured he went a dif'rent route back to give him a chance of runnin' into a fresh batch of recruits. It wasn't long before I saw him pull his next con. There were a half-dozen young kids with dirty faces, hangin' around in front of a convenience store just talkin'. They were dif'rent kids that hung around Coen's, but they had the same world-weary look as Sam and Dadge.

Hi walked by. I swear, he jostled his cart real fast to make all the bells hangin' on it jingle all the more. Then, after he got the kids to look his way, he gave it a sharp twist, causin' two or three things from the top to fall on the sidewalk.

"Look," said the youngest girl, "it's Santa Claus!" She went right over and picked up one of the fallen toys.

"You dropped this," she said timid, like she was a little afraid. "I think it broke."

Well, you guessed it. Before I knew it, Hi was tellin' all the kids about what he was doin' with all the broken toys and makin' promises to 'em that they were goin' to get one special thing their hearts desired this Christmas. Those kids came to life as if they were fed caffeine and sugar and let loose in a toy store. The little girl's eyes couldn't have opened any wider. She

was so happy to hear his promises, you'd think she was tryin'
to pet the fur right off'a Dancer.

I was sick of it. I had enough of Hi and his connin' so I left.
It was gettin' on to noon anyway, and time for me to head over
to Coen's for lunch. I decided I'd take one last trip first, by
goin' out of my way close to Jake's buildin'. I took a route past
the thrift store I thought Hi worked in. It was the only one I
knew of that was three blocks from Jake's. I wanted to check to
see if he really had a job. I expected the folks in the store to say
he worked there, but tell me that he didn't get there 'til some-
time in the afternoon. I felt like the world's biggest chump
goin' in askin' for Hi. Then, when I described him they said,
"You must mean the man who picks things from our trash."

I left steamin' mad.

CHAPTER 11. SAM'S MOTHER GRACE IS SICK. END OF OCTOBER

A couple of weeks went by. It was the Saturday just before Halloween. I went in Coen's for lunch and sat down at one of the few tables they had, so I could eavesdrop on the latest. Dadge was the only one of the kids there at first. Leah came up and put her arm around Dadge's shoulder. He let her for once, instead of pullin' away like usual.

"Dadge, tell me. What has happened to Vic? We never see him anymore."

"Vic has things to do, Mrs. C. That's all."

"Does that mean he's getting into trouble? Because I hear he's up to no good."

"He got arrested, but he got out right away."

"Arrested? What did he do?"

"He stole a car that's all."

"Stole a car? How can you say that's all? Stealing a car is very serious. Dadge, promise me, you'll stay away from him. I can tell you're a good boy. Don't spend time with Vic, or you'll end up to be just like him."

"Alright, Mrs. C., I promise."

Max was half listenin' from behind the counter. He was angry about Sam missin' school so much lately, so he walked over to the table to weigh in.

"You hear what Leah says to you?" Max lectured. "You should listen to her. Vic is headed for prison, sure as the sun will come up tomorrow. He doesn't like anyone to tell him what to do. In prison, they tell you what to do all the day long. You tell him I said that!"

"Listen Dadge," Leah continued, "don't you think Sam and Pauly look up to you? I know they do. What are they going to think if they see you in trouble with the law?"

"I'm not gonna get into any trouble, Mrs. C."

"Already Sam is starting to miss school," Leah went on. "She sees you skipping school, so she thinks that's fine for her. You have to set an example. You want them to grow up right, don't you? So do what's right, and they'll follow and do right themselves. You don't have to talk to them or tell them what to do. If you do right, they'll do right. Understand?"

"Okay, Mrs. C, I'll make sure Sam goes to school."

"You go, too! This is between us," she said, and then she went back to the counter.

"Hey Mr. C., can I have a ham sandwich today?"

"How many times do I have to tell you. There's no ham here. This is a kosher delicatessen."

"But *why* don't you sell it?"

"To be kosher means you love God, and you follow his ways."

"But why is it bad to eat ham? It tastes good and I like it!"

"It's the hoof, the foot of the animal. If it's split like this," he made out with his fingers, "I can't explain it to you! How about a chicken salad sandwich and some coleslaw?"

After Max had stopped tryin' to explain about the ham and made the kid his sandwich, Sam and Pauly came in. Pauly ran up to Leah holdin' a picture he drew in one hand and hangin' onto Half-a Bear with the other as usual.

"Hello, my bubala!" said Leah as she leaned down to give Pauly a kiss. "What do you have there?"

"It's a picture. I drew it! It's for you!"

"Thank you! I'll put it right up on the wall so everybody can see. And how are you today, Sam?"

"Okay," she replied real sad.

"Sam's getting a new coat," Pauly proclaimed. "Mr. Angel said so."

I couldn't help but chime in, "Mr. Engle says a lot of things."

"That's what he says," replied Sam. "He says I'm gonna get a new coat for Christmas because I don't have a real warm one."

"That Mr. Engle," Leah said to me, "I don't know if I like that man or not. He shouldn't make promises to the children like that."

"He's Santa Claus," said Pauly. "Everybody says so. Dancer's his reindeer."

"Who's ev'rybody?" I said. "The other kids?"

"Yeah. He's gonna get everybody just what they want," said Pauly.

"I bet."

"Poet," said Leah with kindness, "let's not say any more right now. Maybe we should wait until after the holidays."

"Maybe he'll get me what I want… a razor to cut my throat - so I don't have to hear any more of Hi's promises."

"Poet, the children."

"Alright, Leah. It's just that the man shouldn't play like he's Santa Claus 'less he can come across with the goods. Sam, don't get your hopes up. Christmas day, he'll prob'ly hand you somethin' he pulled out of a dumpster."

"He has a job," said Max.

"I'm not so sure about that," I said under my breath.

"Maybe he'll buy something from the thrift store where he works, with his own money," said Max. "Let's not be too hasty."

"Well, *I* like him," said Sam. "And if *he* doesn't get me a new coat this year, nobody will."

"Why do you say that?" asked Leah.

"Nothing."

"Sam's mom's sick. That's why," said Pauly.

"Pauly," Sam said reprimandin' him. "I told you not to tell."

"She coughs all the time and lies on the sofa 'cause she's tired," said Pauly.

"I'll fix you up some soup to take to her," said Leah. "You give it to your mother and tell her I hope she's feeling better soon."

After the kids had eaten and taken off, Leah talked to Max real quiet. "I worry about Sam. She's so thin. I wonder if her mother is too sick to earn money – even though we all know what she does for a living. Still, I hope she gets better. You don't mind about the soup, do you Max?"

"You should feed every family in the neighborhood for free," he said in a good-natured way. "Why not? What do we need with money except to pay our bills? You should maybe feed Santa Claus and give his dog a bone while you're at it."

"I know you're joking, but that's a good idea. I think I *will* give his dog a nice bone next time I see him. The dog looks thin."

"If that dog's thin," I said, "it's 'cause it's losin' weight pullin' that fool cart around ev'ry day. I can tell you for a fact: that dog gets more to eat than *I* do. Hi has ev'rybody in the whole damn city feedin' it!"

CHAPTER 12. BRANDT AND CONNIE.
END OF OCTOBER

*A*fter lettin' off some more steam complainin' about Hi, I cruised around for a while and then I went to see Brandt. He's the guy I buy my product from. I us'ally hit his place ev'ry day about three. This time I got there by two 'cause I was so mad about Hi I guess I needed to get someplace. I buy enough from Brandt to sell that same ev'nin'. Jubba doesn't let anybody sell in his territory 'less they pay tribute. Brandt's got this thing goin' with Jubba, where he sells a little to a lot of small-time dealers like me. When one of us hooks somebody regular who starts buyin' big, we have to turn that customer over to one of Jubba's men. Brandt keeps a steady trade and doesn't have to give anything to Jubba 'cept for heavy-duty users we dig up.

Brandt's as cool as they come. He doesn't talk much, and when he does it's real slow. You'd think he was sleepin' most of the time 'cept his eyes are open. He sells product, mostly to make sure he has enough to feed his habit and then some.

He lives on the top floor in an apartment buildin'. It's a loft
with most of the walls knocked out to make one big room.
He's got stuff in there like I've never seen before. He's got his
own bar, like from a Western, with a mirrored back with
shelves filled with liquor bottles. There's a paintin' of a naked
lady done on velvet hangin' over the middle of it. He's got rugs
made from old animal hides like bear and zebra, and a chair
made up from Texas steer horns with the seat covered with
buffalo hides. I never went into his bedroom, but I hear he
sleeps in a brand-new coffin lined with satin. I guess the things
he owns says a lot about him usin' his own product ev'ry day.
Looks like he bought ev'ry one of the strange things in his
place while he was high.

"Hey, man. You're a little early today. You usually stop by
steady as a watch."

"I got off schedule today so I could follow some joker
around."

"He owe you money or somethin'?"

"No. He's a guy I know. He seems like a nice guy, but I
don't know if he is or not. I can't make heads or tails of him."

"What's his name? Maybe I know him."

"His name is Himmel Engel. Folks call him 'Hi'. He goes
around pretendin' to be Santa Claus."

"Oh! I know that dude! Has a dog like a reindeer or somethin'. If he doesn't owe you money, what do you care what he
does?"

"I think he's a liar more than a thief. I've seen him turn
down money folks offered him. I'm wonderin' if he's settin'
'em up to take 'em for a pile later on."

"Sounds like the ways of a confidence man. Makes you

think he's honest at first. Then, when he's got somebody hooked, he reels 'em in for the kill. That's when he makes the big money."

"That's *my* way of thinkin'. Looks like he's settin' up a lot of folks for later. He goes around all day recruitin'."

"What do mean recruitin'?"

"He tricks people into helpin' him lug his cart and buy food for his dog. He put wallets out with money in it, just to talk to folks dumb enough to give it back to him. He's not rakin' in any money now. In fact, don't think he's breakin' even at this point."

"Sometimes a con-man will lose some seed money to rake in a crop of green later on. Whatever it is, I'm guessin' it prob'ly has somethin' to do with Christmas. You know how that time of year makes some people give away their money. This Santa Claus thing he's pushin' is the hook. He's got to be gettin' them all ready for the big day. You wait and see Poet. Lots of suckers will be out a lot of cash come Christmas day, and Santa will ride off to the North Pole where no one can ever find him again," he said laughin'.

"Brandt, I think you're right! I shouldn't get all worked up over this thing, 'cause what you say makes sense. There's somethin' about him makes me think he's up to somethin'. He doesn't seem the type to cheat folks though. If he isn't plannin' on cheatin' folks, I don't know what he's doin'."

"That's what a confidence man *is*. Sounds like he's got you on *his* side. You better watch your money around that old pick pocket."

We talked for a while longer. I started leanin' toward thinkin' Hi was some kind'a crook. It made me feel terrible, so

I cut the conversation short, got my product from Brandt, and went on my way. Brandt and I both thought Hi was out for a big con of some sort. That's what my mind told me anyway. My heart was tryin' to out-shout my mind, sayin' Hi was a good man on a bad mission. I know when it comes to understandin', folks always try to color me with paint from their own brush. It's their mistrustful thoughts that make people turn from me when *I* need help. And it's folks with good hearts that try to see the good in me. I don't think I'm good or bad. I'm just a person gettin' by in a world that feels cold as today's weather.

So, I left Brandt's and went back to my place to rest up for a while. I was too tired to hit up the commuters for donations anyway. Funny, how an empty bed can be somethin' to look forward to when you get old. I thought about gettin' a woman lots of times, and I put the thought right out of my head again. What would an old fart like me want draggin' some disagreeable old lady around with me anyhow? Maybe after she had my heart in her cage, she'd say she didn't want to come with me next time I decided to drift. Anyway, they're always naggin' about somethin' or other. My life's just fine the way it is. 'Cept I do get awfully lonely sometimes. Sometimes I think it even hurts.

I woke up at seven. Just in time to get to my corner to sell my stuff. I took an extra swig before leavin' on account of feelin' sorry for some of the folks I sell my stuff to. I guess gettin' sentimental is part of gettin' old. I often wonder if a trapper feels bad sometimes for the animals he kills just so he can skin 'em.

I had my spot on a corner on the side alley to a liquor store.

Nobody messes with me on account of me havin' Jubba backin' me up – in a roundabout way that is. The alley's dark and cars can run through, stoppin' on the corner long enough for me to sell 'em some dope. I only have weed and some crack. Anybody asks for somethin' else, means I send 'em to the corner where Jubba's dealers do some real biz'ness. Between the liquor store, me, and Connie, it's a full-pleasure corner.

Connie's been workin' this corner with one of her friends for a few years now from what I understand. And you guessed it – Jubba gets his cut. Connie must'a been real cute when she was young, but she's rough trade now. The years have been so hard on her, she looks as if time itself has beaten her up. The lines on her face tell a story that she's been through too much for someone forty years old or thereabout.

I like it when things get slow and we talk. She looks good in the alley shadows, and I like to imagine she's still some young chick who likes talkin' to me. She offers me what she's got in trade for some of my stuff. I told her for certain: "I run a cash-only biz'ness." Besides, I think my merchandise is better than hers when you come right down to it. I never have paid for it anyway.

There was a time when I used to be good lookin'. At least, that's the way I remember it. I don't carry around any pictures of myself. The thing I *do* have is a worn-out old picture of a gal I used to know. I keep it hid in a compartment in my wallet where only I know it's there. I look at it once in a while when I want to drink and feel sorry for myself, wonderin' what my life could'a been like if I'd'a been a dif'rent kind'a man. If I'd'a married her and had some kids. Right now, Connie's the only woman I come close to crossin' paths with.

Tonight, since there wasn't any biz'ness, she came over to shoot the breeze.

"Hey, Poet, how you doin'? Slow night so far," she said. Her voice is low and kind'a scratchy. Cigarettes and alcohol will do that to a person if they keep at it long enough.

"Yeah, it's early yet," I said. "Lot of customers have to get used to the cold. They stay in where it's warm, 'til the devil orders 'em outside. You watch. They'll be out a little later tonight."

"Look at you! You men are so lucky. It's still a man's world. You're out here wearing a coat and pants while I have to walk around in a skirt with the wind blowing up my ass. Poet, you have some candy for your mama?"

"Twenty as usual for you?"

"Is that a special price for me?" she joked.

"I can't say it's a bargain, but I *can* say, I'm not chargin' you more than anybody else."

"You're so generous," she joked again. "Gimmie two this time."

"Here you go," I said, handin' her the poison. "I never remember you buyin' two before. You expectin' company?"

"I need something extra to get me through. You know how it is. Don't you ever use your own stuff?"

"I like to smoke to chill out. I stay away from the rocks. I'm afraid I might get to like it. If ever I *was* gonna use it, tonight would be a good night for it. Say, you ever run into a guy around here playin' Santa Claus?"

"Santa Claus? What's he doing out? They push the holidays earlier every year!"

"No, it's not like that. This isn't a *store* Santa Claus. This is

a guy doin' it on his own. You might'a seen him around somewhere. He's getting' to look a lot like Santa. He has long, white
hair, a white beard, and he's got a dog wearin' antlers, hooked
up to a cart with bells all over it. You tell me you've never seen
him?"

"I don't come out much in the daytime. Unless he hangs
out in bars. That would be the only way I'd see him. What's he
using the get-up for? What kind of game's *he* runnin'?"

"I can't figure him out. He's got all kinds of folks buyin'
into him bein' a nice old man. I figure, somehow in the end,
he's got to have figured out a way to scam those folks out of
money. But I don't know how."

"You know me, Poet, I don't cheat anybody. My customers
get just what they pay for like yours do. But there are plenty of
people out there who *want* to be cheated. They're sitting
around waiting for it. If he isn't hitting up anybody for money
now, maybe he's like a fortune teller. You know; the first visit's
only ten bucks. Then it's fifty to talk to your dead aunt. The
next thing you know, the suckers are shelling out hundreds,
just to be told what they want to hear. Maybe your Santa Claus
is setting everybody up. Maybe he'll hit them all up at the
same time and then skip town. That's what I'd do – if I was
that way."

"That's the general idea I hear when I've asked folks about
him. They think he's gettin' ready for a big kill at Christmas. I
just can't believe he's that kind'a man. And he's old, older than
me. Scams are for young guys who need money for a habit or
gamblin' or somethin'."

"That's nice that you think that way. You have a good heart
– like me. Maybe the guy's straight. Maybe he's crazy or some-

thing. I don't want to burst your bubble. I hope it turns out alright, and the guy's okay."

We chatted a little more. It wasn't long before trade picked up for both of us, and we got back to workin'. Funny how things are. She was the first person hopin'– hopin' that Hi was on the level. I guess she *does* have a good heart.

CHAPTER 13. DADGE AND VIC STEAL A CAR. SECOND WEEK OF NOVEMBER

*A*couple weeks later, Dadge met up with Vic on a Saturday night for somethin' else. Dadge had been gettin' in deeper. He hadn't said no to anything Vic asked him to, up to now. This was the night he was to get jumped for the first time – that is, if he got through what it was he had to do to get in Jubba's gang. It was a cold, dark moonless night about eight o'clock.

"Vic, where we going tonight?" asked Dadge.

"You're followin' me and doin' what I tell you. That's all you need to know. C'mon, we're gonna catch a bus cross town."

"What's that you're carrying? It looks like a doctor's bag."

"There's somethin' real valuable in here we need for tonight. Be cool. Don't be shootin' your mouth off or askin' a lot of questions with people around."

They rode the bus without hardly talkin' just like Vic wanted. Dadge wondered what was about to happen. He looked Vic's coat over when he was sure Vic wasn't lookin', to figure out if he was packin'. Not talkin' was bad for Dadge's nerves. He was gettin' sorry he'd agreed to come along this time. The stakes were gettin' higher, and Dadge knew Jubba had come up with somethin' sketchy since this was his first step to gettin' into the gang. When they got out of the bus, Dadge started askin' questions again.

"Where we goin', Vic?"

"It's not far. What'd I tell you about askin' questions? Tonight's your chance. So, stop actin' like a kid, and step up!"

"I was only asking."

"You know how to steal a car?" asked Vic.

"No, I never did that. You hot wire it. Don't you?"

"That's the way your grandpa did it. I got the latest in the bag. We have to lift a Toyota for a chop shop. Look for a Camry. Can't be more than three years old. One of Jubba's guys has this new way to bust into a car that's smooth. I've been practicin' on cars in a junk yard."

"Is that one on the corner?" asked Dadge.

"That's the right kind, but there're too many people around. Let's go 'round back of the strip club on tenth. That place gets packed on Saturday nights."

The two talked as they walked to the club. Dadge thought ev'ry eye was watchin' him includin' God himself. Vic made car stealin' sound like an ev'ryday thing. If it wasn't for him seemin' like he was at such ease, Dadge would'a backed out for sure. After a while, they found a car in a quiet spot on a back street with bad lightin'.

"There's one," said Vic, "parked back there. Don't worry,

guys stay in the club 'til all their money's gone. Here, put this on."

Vic opened up the bag and threw Dadge a ski mask and put one on himself.

"Do we really need these?"

"There're cameras everywhere. Put it on."

Vic reached in the bag and slapped a big, black rubber suction cup with a handle on it, to the middle of the driver's side window. Then, he pulled out a glass cutter and sliced up and down and across - all around it. After that, he ran tape up all around it.

"The tape holds the glass so it don't make a noise," said Vic. "Soon as break the window, you reach in and pop the hood. The alarm's gonna go off. I'll go in front and cut the wires fast. If somethin' goes wrong, and I tell you to run, take off and don't look back."

But Dadge didn't have to run. It went just like Vic said it would. He pulled on the suction cup handle, and the window made a 'pop', breakin' up the glass into dif'rent size pieces. Easy as that. Vic quick cut the wires and the horn stopped, but the lights kept flashin'. A minute later they were sittin' in the car; Vic in the driver's seat with Dadge lookin' on.

"Here it is," said Vic, openin' up the bag to show Dadge. "All's I have to do is push this button and keep my foot on the brake.

"What is that?"

"It's a computer Jubba paid a ton a money for."

"What's it do?"

"It throws out codes until it hits the one that works the car. When the ignition light's green, I start the car and we're off!

You watch out to see if anyone's comin'. I gotta watch the ignition to see when it flashes."

Two minutes seemed to go on forever for Dadge. Vic seemed to like it. He was smilin' and looked like he was turned on by the idea of stealin' the car.

"There it is! It flashed!"

Vic opened the bag up wide. Dadge gave a good look down in at the black box inside.

"Now, I gotta push *this* button, and it'll play the last few codes back slow. Then I start the car."

The ignition light went on again. Vic started the car and the lights stopped flashin'. The two boys were on their way drivin' down the road; laughin' and excited. Not thinkin' about what might happen if things went south.

"Take your mask off," said Vic. "We're clear!"

"Are we goin' to Jubba's or the chop shop?"

"We got a couple places to go. Jubba's, the chop shop... But first, I got a stop to make. You know how to drive?"

"I never drove a car."

"You gotta drive four blocks, that's all."

"Vic, I can't drive! I don't know how."

"It's only four blocks. All you have to do is hold the wheel straight. There ain't no turns. You know which is the gas and which is the brake. You're *gonna* do it!" Vic yelled, backhandin' him.

Dadge sat there dumbfounded. He didn't like takin' orders and bein' told to shut up and do what he was told. He was startin' to understand what 'goin' down the drain' meant. He felt like he was stuck in somethin' that he was gettin' deeper and deeper down into, without bein' able to get out. He had gone along with ev'rything Vic wanted him to so far. He had shoplifted, snatched a purse, and stood by watchin' Vic beat a guy over the head with a pipe to take his wallet, never knowin' for sure if the man ever got up again. Now he started to wonder if his future was headin' toward prison with no other road.

"We're almost there," said Vic. "When I stop the car, you run around to the driver's side. Put your foot on the brake and don't you move it! You keep it there. Put the car in drive and wait. Don't do nothin'! You just sit here and wait. You got me?"

"Yeah, Vic. I got it."

Vic pulled the car up in front of a convenience store with the passenger side facin' the glass front. Dadge watched Vic pull his ski mask back on while Vic sat there for a while waitin' for the right time. Dadge stopped askin' questions. He felt kind'a numb inside and didn't know what to do but just keep goin'. Then Vic hollered, "C'mon!" and jumped out of the car and ran into the store. Dadge ran around the car and strapped himself into the driver's seat and did what he was told.

Things stopped seemin' real to Dadge. Seein' Vic behind the store window was like he was watchin' a TV show or a movie. Vic pulled a gun out of his jacket and held it high up in the air, pointin' it down at the top of the cashier's head. Dadge heard his heart beat loud as he watched.

Vic looked jumpy and nervous, while the man took money from the register. Dadge saw clear as day through the glass that the robbery wasn't about the money. It was about somethin' else. Maybe power, the way Vic held the gun high up on him. Or excitement, Vic gettin' a rush that was makin' him jittery. Whatever it was, Dadge prayed Vic wouldn't shoot.

A car pulled up for a while and then drove away fast. Dadge knew they'd seen what was goin' on and were prob'ly already callin' the police. No way he could outrun a police car. He didn't even know if he could drive four blocks like Vic told him to. Dadge's mind raced. Then, the time that seemed to drag on long, ended. Vic made the man lie down behind the counter and then he ran out the door and jumped in the car.

"Hit the gas!"

Vic grabbed the wheel from the passenger side and tore off his mask. The car tires squealed as the car peeled out onto the street.

"Go! Go! Go! Don't stop till I tell ya!"

They swerved around a few cars on the street.

"Let up on the gas. Slow down now. Over there!" Vic said, pointin' at the next block.

Dadge was so nervous, that when Vic yelled "Stop!" he jammed on the brakes. They both pushed on the dashboard to keep from hittin' their heads on it. Vic grabbed hold of the shift and popped the car in park. "Get out!" he yelled. And they both got out to switch places again. After they were back in, Vic started to drive away slow and easy.

"How come you're goin' so slow? We're gonna get caught!"

"Jubba's guys showed me. You gotta blend right in. If you start speedin', the cops will know *this* car is the one they're after. Did you see the look on that guy's face when I had the gun on him? I thought he'd shit!" he said laughin'.

"Yeah, I saw the whole thing. I thought you were gonna shoot."

"I was told not to, no matter what. That's a real mean gun I got. It's a Smith & Wesson 40. One shot put right and it's over. Soon as I'm in, I get my own gun."

Dadge listened to Vic talk as they drove the rest of the way. Dadge told me later – the more Vic tried to sound like a man talkin' about stealin' and hurtin', and gettin' in the gang, the more he sounded like a fool. Dadge sure did need *somethin'* in his life, but he didn't want *regret* to be it.

CHAPTER 14. VIC AND DADGE GET BEAT UP AT JUBBA'S. SECOND WEEK OF NOVEMBER

A few minutes later they pulled up to a run-down garage in the burbs. Vic honked three times and a bay door opened. After they drove in, the door closed behind 'em and Dadge jumped out of the car. He was happy to be out – 'til he saw the same two muscle men that had brought him and Vic to Jubba's a couple months before. They *weren't* glad to see him. They were the kind'a guys who never joked.

"I see you got the goods like you was supposed to," one said. "We got the rig out back."

They followed the two men to the tripped-out Cadillac and the two men pushed 'em into the car real rough.

"Are we goin' to Jubba's now?" Dadge asked.

The only thing the guy ridin' in the back said was, "Give me your phones and shut up!"

It was the same drill as before. The two boys had to put blindfolds on. When they got to the place, they were dragged up the stairs, then ordered to take off the masks. They were in the large room with a dozen men, Raphael and Anthony were there with 'em, and Jubba was sittin' in his chair.

"Everything go right?" Jubba asked one of the muscle men.

"Yes, sir. They got the goods."

"Okay then," he said as if he didn't care.

Jubba's chair creaked somethin' fierce as he pulled himself out of it to stand. He took his cigar along with him as he walked up to the boys. He got right in Vic's face blowin' smoke at him.

"You think you're tough enough to be one of my men?

"Yes, sir. I think…"

Before Vic could finish, Jubba sucker-punched him in the gut, makin' Vic double over. Then he got up in Dadge's face. "What about you? You tough?"

"Yes, sir," he said soundin' like he was braggin' to make sure he didn't sound scared.

Dadge stared right back at Jubba without flinchin'. Jubba turned and sat back in his chair without even layin' a hand on him.

"You!" Jubba yelled, pointin' at Vic with the butt end of his cigar. "You can fight back if you want to. Your friend has to take what *he* gets. Let's see how tough you two are. Let's start this thing! Don't beat the new guy to death. It's his first time."

The men couldn't wait to lay hurt on 'em. At the head of the line for dishin' out were Anthony and Raphael. Raphael and the other guys, picked up sticks, while Anthony grabbed a heavy chain. Raphael beat Vic harder than anybody, to show he wasn't takin' it easy just 'cause he knew the guy.

It was purely recreation for the men. Their time to give what they had all received, to get where they were. They let their anger out with satisfaction in ev'ry blow. They hit the two with sticks and punched 'em. Raphael beat 'em with sticks and kicked 'em when they were down. Vic fought well. He laid on a few good punches at first. The fight was nothin' about bein' fair, it was about beatin' down the new guys... so two or three against one was the way it went down. The beatin's had been goin' on for more than ten minutes when Anthony started in with his chain. That thing could crack ribs... and it did. Anthony got a big kick out of that.

Dadge stood up real well under it all. Course, they weren't dishin' it out so hard to him as they were to Vic. Dadge was just gettin' a taste. They were both used to gettin' beatin's at home anyway. He got knocked down sure enough, and when he got right back up, the expression on his face said he could take it.

It was hard for Dadge to watch the chain bein' takin' to Vic, as he was bein' beatin' down to stay down. Vic got it across the back and on his chest as Raphael kicked him around the floor.

"Okay," said Jubba. "Give 'em a little more and wrap it up. They've had enough."

The men got their last licks in real good. They weren't gonna let weaklings in the gang. New guys would have to watch their backs like ev'rybody else, so they made sure Vic was tough enough to take it. Raphael gave Dadge a good punch square in the face, which might'a broken his nose. Then Anthony whacked Vic a couple more times hard with the chain.

"They done real good," said Jubba. "I like the new guy. Give him a good one with chain Ant'ny. I wanna see how he takes it."

So, Raphael gut-punched Dadge and pushed him to the floor. Anthony whipped him once hard with the chain. The chain wrapped around the back of his ribs snappin' him hard. The boys were both layin' on the ground groanin' when Jubba gave the word.

"That's it. They done real good. Take 'em back now."

"C'mon," said the driver, and picked Vic up by the arm makin' him stand. "You can cry when you get home."

"Come on, Dadge," commanded Vic. "Get yourself up. You're not hurt bad."

Vic was pleased with himself for takin' all he was given. He didn't smile though. He knew this was no place to show emotion of any kind; not in front of all of Jubba's men.

It was a long ride home, cracked ribs and all. This time, they got dropped off in their own neighborhood.

"You alright, Vic?" Dadge asked as the car pulled away.

Soon as the car was out of sight Dadge wiped the blood from under his nose, and Vic put his arm around Dadge's shoulder to hold himself up.

"That was somethin' else," Vic said, holdin' onto his ribs with his other hand. "That sure was hard to take. I'm as good as in now."

"I'm not sure if I want to get in," said Dadge.

"Hey man, Jubba's gang is right for guys like us. I seen how your brother is. You say your old man is like that too?"

"Yeah, he's even worse."

"Okay then. You *need* somebody backin' you up. You moved up tonight. Jubba likes your style. Everybody could see that. You're like my brother. You keep it up – pretty soon the whole gang will be your family."

"I'm not sure that's what I want."

Vic stood up on his own and poked around his ribs to figure out which ones were hurtin' the most.

"What'a you want to be alone on the streets?"

"I don't know. It just seems like I'm gettin' it worse being around those guys."

"Those guys are tough. That's why they gotta jump us in – to make sure we're as tough as they are. After I'm in, it'll be dif'rent. Ain't nobody gonna lift a finger against me, not even my old man."

"I don't need a gang. I can take care of myself."

Vic leaned on Dadge again, and the two started walkin'.

"You get a little older," said Vic, "someday your old man's gonna throw you out. Then where'll you be?"

"I guess."

"You'll be nowhere, *that's* where. You'll be nothin'! Listen, we been together since grade school. You stick and we're gonna have all those guys to hang with forever. We'll have money and cars and *nobody'll* mess with us!"

Dadge did some heavy thinkin' after that night. He wasn't sold on the idea of joinin' the gang 'cause he kept wonderin' if he was just tradin' one bad family for another.

CHAPTER 15. PAULY'S LEFT ALONE. FIRST WEEK OF DECEMBER

Thanksgivin' had come and gone along with November. Dadge kept his promise to stay in school. He did at least, most of the time. Sam followed his lead and made sure Pauly went ev'ry day. She'd duck out sometimes though after she delivered Pauly in through the doors. One mornin' in the beginnin' of December, Sam went to walk Pauly to school and found him shiverin' outside his place.

"Pauly, what are you doing out here?" she asked. The little guy was hunched on the back steps of his buildin' shakin' like a hurt puppy.

"What's the matter?"

Pauly said somethin', but Sam couldn't hear him 'cause he had his face buried in Half-a Bear. I don't guess this was the first time that sad bear sopped up Pauly's tears.

"I can't understand you," Sam said real kind. "You have your bear in front of your face."

"I couldn't get in," he said wipin' his face with the bear.

"What do you mean? Isn't anyone home?"

"They're gone," he said sobbin'.

"There must be somebody there. Come on... Let's go see."

Sam opened the door to the apartment buildin' leadin' Pauly by the hand. They walked down the old carpet in the hall, all flat in the middle where the rug was worn down to the bottom. It was seven in the mornin' and most people were in their apartments gettin' ready for the day ahead. They could hear all the hustle and bustle 'til they got in front of Pauly's apartment door.

Sam grabbed hold of the old brass doorknob, givin' it a hard twist. She tried it a couple more times, then she crouched down and looked through the keyhole.

"There's nobody there," said Pauly, startin' to cry again.

Sam looked long and hard before sayin' anything.

"I don't see anybody. Maybe your mom's sick or something, and I just can't see her."

"No," said Pauly, hangin' his head and draggin' Half-a Bear as he went walkin'away. "Nobody's there."

"How do you know she's gone? She could be fallin' down sick."

"She's not sick. She's gone."

Pauly went outside and took his place on the back steps again. Sam gave one last look through the keyhole before finally givin' up. Then she went outside and sat down next to Pauly on the back steps.

"She went away. I heard them."

"Who's them? You mean your mom and her boyfriend?"

"They thought I was asleep but I wasn't."

"What did they say?"

"He said he was going away. He didn't want to take care of somebody else's kid. They had a big fight."

"Then what?"

"He left, and Mommy cried."

"So maybe she went to stay with him. You know, until he leaves for the other town."

"She's gone," he said, cryin' into Half-a Bear.

"Don't cry. She'll come back. Give her a chance."

They sat together for a few minutes more. Sam put her arm around him and sat quiet 'til Pauly stopped cryin'.

"I've got an idea. You can come home with me. My mom lays on the sofa most of the time now. I could sneak you into my room and you can climb out the window when it's time for school. We'll come back here every day until your mommy comes home. I'll write a note and slip it under the door for her, so she knows where you are."

"You're only saying that to be nice. Mommy's never coming back. I know she isn't."

"She'll come back. You'll see. Wouldn't you like to come to my house?"

"Your mommy wouldn't mind?"

"We won't tell her. She sleeps most of the time. We'll keep each other company."

CHAPTER 16. SAM'S MOTHER GRACE IS VERY SICK. SAM AND PAULY VISIT HI. SECOND WEEK OF DECEMBER

I didn't know about the goin's on between Pauly and Sam, or even about Max and Amir havin' coffee together. I found out about those things in the beginnin' of the new year, after the bus'ness with Hi was over.

Sam kept makin' sure Pauly went to school ev'ry day and hid him out at her place at night. Her mother Grace was terrible ill and didn't catch on right away. Sam went to school most of the time. Dadge wasn't skippin' so much as he used to. And well, Vic, he never had gone back since the start of the school year.

It was the first week of December and gettin' colder ev'ry day. Things had been runnin' along the same for a while. Vic was runnin' down the road toward a life a crime; Dadge was thinkin' hard about walkin' away from it. Sam was gettin' tired and worn out – havin' to be too grown up for a little girl. It was gettin' near impossible for her to take care of Pauly and her mother, never mind lookin' after herself.

Sam's mother Grace, was sick on the sofa 24/7. Dadge came over once in a while to check up on things. He'd slip Sam a few bucks when he could. Sam and Pauly had breakfast and lunch at school, so they weren't starvin'. The Coens were givin' 'em sandwiches ev'ry day after school. Grace wasn't makin' a dime and she needed to eat too. So, Sam started savin' her food up to give to her. It wasn't long that Pauly stopped bein' a secret. His spirit was too big to keep hidden in a corner of an apartment. Grace was weak from bein' sick to object to him stayin' there.

"I want to see Santa!" Pauly yelled in excitement to Sam.

"There aren't any Santas in the stores around here," Grace explained in a whisper. That was the loudest her sickness would let her talk.

"No! Santa that has Dancer," Pauly whispered back to her.

"I don't know where he is," said Sam, pullin' him away so her sick mother could rest. "Nobody does. He walks around all day."

"I want a baseball glove, a ball, *and* a bat. I have to tell him so he'll have them for Christmas."

"I don't think he can get those things for you, honey. He's not the real Santa," Sam explained.

"He is too Santa. He has a reindeer and everything! Dancer's gonna turn into a real reindeer on Christmas Eve. Then Mr. Angel will fly in the sky and give presents out. Look!" he said holdin' up his bear. "Half-a Bear wants to see him too. Can we go see him? Can we?"

"Alright. I guess it doesn't matter if we're a little late for school. I think I know the store where he works."

So, Sam walked quick with Pauly in tow. Walkin' fast was

one sure way for Sam to try to keep warm. She loved the boy, so she had a hard time sayin' no to a kid who only wanted what most kids his age ask for: a chance to tell Santa what they want. About fifteen blocks later, Sam and Pauly were pressin' their faces up against the ice-cold glass of the darkened store.

"The sign says the store doesn't open 'til nine. That's almost an hour. We can't wait here all that time. It's freezing out," said Sam.

"I know where he lives," said Pauly.

"How would you know where he lives?" Sam asked, almost scoldin' him.

"Kids leave letters for him there. That's what I wanna do."

"Well, where is it?"

"I don't know where it is, but I know how to get there."

"You mean you don't know the address."

"Yes. I don't know the address. Can we go?" he asked, beggin'.

Pauly put on the biggest smile he could. He stuck his finger in his mouth and began swayin' back and forth. He was just too cute to say no to.

"Now, we'll be late for school *and* we'll miss breakfast. Are you sure you know how to get there?"

"I've been there twice with other kids, but I didn't go in."

"Well, alright. I guess it won't hurt to try."

Truth be told, Sam wanted to believe in old Hi the way Pauly did, but she was too familiar with the disappointments of life to be as innocent. She thought maybe she'd feel dif'rent by walkin' up to Santa's house. Anyway, she thought she'd give it a go.

It was a long walk to Santa's house, or maybe I'll just say

Jake's apartment buildin'. 'Cause of the thin cloth makin' up her coat Sam was shiverin' by the time they laid eyes on the front stoop. She was so cold, she was just shy of havin' her teeth chatterin'. Pauly ran around the side of the buildin' into the alley and stood starin' up.

"There it is!" yelled Pauly, pointin' up to the seventh-floor fire escape. That's Santa's house!"

There were red and green blinkin' lights on all the windows of the corner apartment. There were wreaths hung from the outside of each of the windows, and green, red, and gold garland wrapped all along the fire escape railin' with red and green glass ornaments hangin' down.

"You see? I told you."

"That looks like it alright. I'm frozen."

"I'm twice as frozed."

"We may as well go in to get warm anyway."

The two of 'em pulled on the front door handle to open the heavy, old, wood door. As quiet as they tried to be, the door creaked somethin' fierce. Their footsteps were like the sound was turned up, as the echoes from their shoes wound around inside the buildin'. They tried to be quiet walkin' on the hard tile floor, but they weren't.

"These mailboxes are just like the ones in our building," said Sam. "And there are the bells," she said, pointin' to the panel with all the push-buttons.

"That's his!" Pauly yelled. He didn't notice the mailbox had the name 'Engel' written in pencil behind the dirty glass window on it. It was the red and green stickers of Christmas trees and wreaths that gave it away.

"I feel funny ringin' somebody's bell when we're not

invited. I wonder which one it is?" Sam said, starin' at the panel with all the push-buttons. "There's no number on the mailbox."

Just then they jumped from bein' startled.

"Hey, you kids."

Old Jake was standin' there behind 'em big as ever. They stood still, like a pair of reindeer caught in the headlights.

"You two lookin' for Santa Claus?"

"Yeah," Sam said, amazed that such a rough-lookin' character knew what they were doin'.

"I'm gonna give him a letter," said Pauly.

"I'm takin' his letters."

"We didn't write one yet," said Sam.

"No problem. Santa has all that stuff. You go see him, and after, you can slip the letter under my door. Okay?"

Jake looked more like a big ogre than a Christmas elf. Somethin' in his voice made 'em feel safe.

"Don't you think it's kind of early? Maybe he's sleeping or something," said Sam.

"He's up already. You ain't the first kids here today. Go on. He likes it when people come to see him – especially kids. Go on. It's alright."

Pauly's shorter legs moved that much faster than Sam's. He raced up the flights of stairs with Sam chasin' after him. He was drawn like a magnet to Hi's door – like he already knew where it was. Just like most kids who want to see Santa, Pauly's courage melted away when he stood in front of the door.

"Remember, Pauly, he's not Santa Claus, so don't call him that. Call him Mr. Engle."

"Alright. But he *is* Santa."

Three raps was all it took to bring Hi to open the door.

"Well, hello, Sam and Pauly. What a nice surprise. Come on in!"

Dancer greeted the guests with barks, and he licked their faces like they were lollipops.

"Hi, Mr. Angel," Pauly said grinnin'.

"It's Engle, not 'Angel', Pauly," Sam corrected.

The two visitors didn't judge Hi; they were there to see him. They *did* have to walk through a maze of pathways in Hi's place to navigate past the ocean of junk that was at high tide. Dancer had lots of practice walkin' amongst it. He was nimble and knew where to step, so he wouldn't knock the piles over.

"Look at it all!" exclaimed Pauly. "I never saw so much Christmas stuff – ever."

"You sure do have a lot of decorations, Mr. Engle. Are you going to hang these all up?"

"Oh yes, I certainly am. I enjoy Christmas so much. I never seem to have enough decorations. I wish the holiday lasted all year long. Then I'd never have to take them down. I have string upon string of lights – all different kinds. And decorations – boxes and boxes of them and so much tinsel!"

Hi was like a regular old pirate showin' off all his treasure to the kids. He held up dif'rent strings of lights like they were pearl necklaces. He handed his favorite ornaments over for the two kids to admire; handlin' 'em like they were crowns of gold.

"Wow, Mr. Angel. Where did you get all this?" asked Pauly.

"That's what my cart is for. Dancer and I bring these in from all over the city."

After a while, the youngster couldn't hold back from askin' the question he just had to know the answer to.

"Are you really Santa Claus, Mr. Angel?"

"Well, Pauly, I never said I *was* Santa. I may look like him a little bit, and I do like to give out presents. Come into the other room. Wait until I show you all the wonderful toys and things I'm fixing up for all the children. Come in. Let me show you."

They followed him into a dark room. He flicked on the light. There around 'em were broken things, and boxes full'a broken things, piled around all the walls up to the ceilin'. The two kids clung on to each other as they looked up at the mountains around 'em.

"You see!" said Hi. "Look at all these wonderful things. I'm going to fix all these broken toys up just like new. Every child will get exactly what they want this Christmas. You wait and see!"

Hi dug into one of the piles startin' a minor avalanche.

"Here's the skateboard I'm going to fix up for Dadge! Wait until he sees this after I'm through with it. Will he be surprised!"

Pauly's spirits couldn't be dampened. To his young eyes, he was in a regular wonderland. After Hi handed the broken skateboard to Sam, she looked the hopeless thing over with confusion. She couldn't help but love the old man, but she had no idea how one person could'a ever fix up the mountain of broken things in time for Christmas.

"And Pauly, I know what you want for Christmas. I didn't forget."

"There's something else I want too."

"I have a pencil and paper here someplace. You can write a letter to Santa."

"Aren't *you* Santa Claus?" asked Pauly.

"Just because somebody wears a baseball cap, that doesn't mean they play ball for a living. Lots of people do things they enjoy because they like to. Remember, I never said I was Santa."

Pauly tilted his head like a puzzled puppy. He couldn't figure out what Hi just said – whether he *was* or *wasn't* Santa.

"The man downstairs told us to give letters for Santa to him," said Sam.

"That's right. You can both sit down and write letters to Santa and leave them with the man in 1A. He's one of the people who's helping."

Sam helped Pauly write just the right letter to Santa. When they were done, Hi gave 'em each an envelope and told 'em how to make out the address to the North Pole.

"What about you, Sam? Aren't you going to write a letter to Santa?"

"No. I'm fine. I don't need anything."

"You can always write a letter up to Christmas Eve. You know where to leave it in case you change your mind."

"I don't think so. I'm glad you like Christmas so much. Merry Christmas, Mr. Engle."

"Merry Christmas, Mr. Angel!"

Pauly skipped down the seven flights, slippin' his letter under Jake's door on the way out.

"Isn't he Santa?" Pauly asked as they were leavin' the buildin'.

"He looks like Santa alright."

"He *must* be. He wouldn't have all those Christmas things if he wasn't. And he has Dancer!"

The two were very late for school that day. Pauly couldn't stop talkin' about Hi and all the things in his apartment. There was no stoppin' him. He told ev'ry kid in his class about his visit and then some.

CHAPTER 17. MORE COFFEE WITH AMIR, MAX, AND POET. SECOND WEEK OF DECEMBER

*W*ith Christmas only two weeks away, things were gettin' worse. Hi had gotten to look a lot like Santa would'a looked – if Santa had gone crazy that is. I don't think the man cut or combed his hair since he first came to town. I hadn't yet seen him with one fixed-up toy, and there wasn't one kid who needed some carin' for who wasn't promised somethin'.

I was in Coen's eatin' lunch, and Leah was talkin' on her phone real familiar like she was talkin' to a friend. I heard her say, "It's nice of you to invite us to dinner. Of course, we'll come." Well, Max must'a heard her 'cause just then I saw him sneakin' around. While Leah kept talkin' with all smiles and bein' real chatty, Max picked up a towel and made like he was cleanin' the back of the display cases. He polished and walked sideways 'til he worked himself right near her. Then, he leaned one ear in to do some good old-fashioned eavesdroppin'. When Leah was through talkin', Max started rubbin' the cases faster and walkin' the other way. Leah said somethin' to him. Must'a been somethin' about what she was talkin' about.

Max smiled and nodded and then real quick, threw down the towel and headed out the door. He tapped on the front window of Amir's shop and waved 'til Amir came outside.

"Max, what is it?" Amir asked. "You're so early. Did something happen?"

"Amir, our wives have been talking. Is this something you know about?"

"Yes, Max. Zara told me she was going to invite you and Leah to dinner. I said it was fine and promised not to say anything until she asked you."

"I see. Well, of course, I have nothing against it. It's fine with me also. I can understand that our wives talked to each other first. Why should anyone talk to me? After all, some women think talking to each other is so important, second only to praying to God."

"It wasn't my idea either. But now that plans have been made, we shouldn't make trouble. I'm glad our wives get along so well."

"Why shouldn't they get along? They're both good people. I don't expect your wife Zara should know how to cook kosher. Not that every, single, thing has to be kosher."

"Truth is, I'll be making most of the dishes. I enjoy cooking."

"So, then *you* know how to cook kosher?"

"No Max, of course not. I'll cook, but I'm not in charge of the menu. This is something Zara and Leah will have to work out. I suggest we don't get involved in the politics of it. Let them come up with a plan, and lets you and I will enjoy the food... and the company, too, of course."

"Of course, the company," said Max. "We can't stand out here all day in the cold. Maybe some coffee would be good to warm us up. Why don't you come into our store? We can have some normal... What I mean to say is American coffee. Not that your coffee isn't good. It is."

"I know what you mean, Max."

"Sometimes I think coffee should taste like coffee. It's only right."

I bet if I had taken a seat in a dif'rent spot at Coen's that day, I'd never have been invited. But when Max walked in, he happened to be starin' me right in the face. Bein' that he was with Amir, he must'a felt funny about lookin' at me without knowin' what to say.

"Poet," he said, pausin' like he was tryin' to come up with somethin', "Come in the back room with us. I'd like you should have coffee with us. You can bring your lunch with you."

"Sure, Max. That sounds good to me."

I was followin' Amir when I walked through the curtains into the backroom for the first time. We all sat down at the old red and white enamel table, me sittin' across from Max. I set my lunch down in front of me, givin' a quick look around. So, there I was, sittin' with two business owners – just the three of us.

"You know Poet, don't you, Amir?"

"I've seen him many times, but we've never been introduced. It's good to meet you."

"It's good to meet you, Amir. I've seen you around the neighborhood and by your store, of course."

"What's new, Poet? Have you been busy?" asked Max.

"Trade is always strong before the holidays. Lots of folks alone. Always need a little somethin' to pick 'em up."

I turned to Amir and clued him in. "I sell a little product down by the liquor store. Nothin' harmful you understand."

"That's alright, Poet. I'm not judgmental. Business is the same for me. In my store, it's for Christmas presents. Wives and girlfriends buying cigars for their men, you know."

"Speakin' of Christmas, have either of you seen our local Santa Claus lately? You know Hi, don't you, Amir?"

"You can't help but know him," said Max.

Max got up and started makin' coffee.

"If you don't see him, you hear him with all those bells," he said.

"If you haven't seen him by now," I said, "chances are, you won't see him after Christmas."

"Yes, I've seen him many times with his dog," said Amir. "Why is he trying to look like that I wonder?"

"Why do you say that, Poet?" asked Max. "You don't think he's going to the North Pole after he delivers all the presents, do you?" he said with a laugh.

"Me and a few other folks, think our friendly neighborhood Santa is nothin' but an old con-man. We think he's prob'ly buildin' up for a big score. I'm thinkin' he's gonna hit a lot of folks up for money sayin' he's gonna use it to buy presents for kids. Ev'rybody knows he's made promises to kids all over the city. If he tells folks he doesn't have time to fix all that junk he's been haulin' around, they'll shell out to stop all those kids from cryin' on Christmas mornin'."

"I don't think so, Poet. I know Hi is a little crazy walking around looking like he does, but he's always been nice to the children. They all love him."

"You better be ready to give out handkerchiefs to Sam and Pauly for presents, 'cause they'll be cryin' for sure. Those two don't need any more sorrows than they got already. You know Pauly's had no place to live for some time now."

"How can a child have no place to live?" asked Amir. "Are his parents homeless?"

"He never had a father around as far as I know, and his mother picked up and left after meetin' another man is what I heard."

"That's horrible," said Amir. "How could someone do something like that? Where does he live? A boy could freeze to death in this cold."

"Yes, Poet. Where does he live if he's got no place?" asked Max.

"Sam's taken him in. She's been sneakin' him in ev'ry day after school. That's gettin' easier to do, what with Sam's mother Grace at death's door."

"Grace," Max said hushed to Amir, "is a woman of the street."

"The poor kids would have nothin' to eat if it wasn't for you two, Max. I've been slippin' Sam a few bucks now and then myself, to make sure they don't run short. I wouldn't be surprised if Sam's been givin' most her food to Grace."

"I think we should call someone," said Amir.

"I'd hold off on that if I were you," I told 'em. "Sam's goin' through enough these days. It'd be wrong to take her away from her dyin' mother just yet. And Pauly's no worse off now than he was before."

"You're right," said Max. "Now isn't the time," he said, reachin' in his pocket. Then he stuffed a couple of twenties in my hand. "Be sure they have what they need."

"I sure will, Max."

"Here's mine, Poet," said Amir, doin' the same.

I couldn't believe those two trusted me so much – forkin' over money to me, just like that. That was the most respected I felt in years.

"I don't know what'll happen after Grace dies," I went on. "That'll be the time to call somebody for sure. Guess those two will end up stuck in the system. Pauly's young enough to get adopted out. Sam, I don't know. Guess she'll go from foster home to foster home, like what happened to me."

The coffee finished brewin' and we all went on talkin' for a while. Wished I had better news to share with those two. Seems bad news always comes in bunches.

CHAPTER 18. DINNER WITH AMIR. THIRD WEEK OF DECEMBER

*I*t was December the twentieth, only five days 'til Christmas when the Coens took a visit to Amir and Zara's apartment. It hadn't snowed yet for the season. It was close to freezin' and pitch-black out by six-thirty, so Max and Leah took a cab the twelve blocks over.

"Don't worry, Mama," said Max. "I won't say anything."

"But I *am* worried. After all, this is the first time we're eating in a gentile house. There may be dishes you won't be accustomed to," said Leah as they rode along. "I helped Zara to understand what kosher food is. Who knows if she could learn so fast?"

"Whatever it is they put in front of me, how bad could it be? I'll eat it."

"I'm not saying it will be bad. I'm telling you they use different spices. Some things may taste differently than we're used to. Different, that's all I'm saying."

"Alright, so the food will be different. I promise you Mama, whatever they put in front of me I'll eat, so long as it doesn't stare back at me. I'm not going to eat anything with a head on it still."

"Maxie, don't be foolish. Barbarians they're not. Amir and Zara are very refined people. I'm sure everything will be fine. I just don't want you to make a fuss, that's all I'm saying. Maybe they'll even put in front of us something that isn't kosher."

"Fuss? I never make a fuss. I'll maybe ask a question. I don't want to eat something if I don't know what it is."

"Fine, ask a question. Just don't make a fuss. Better yet, don't ask a question. It's better tonight if you use your mouth for eating than for asking. The main thing is, they're good people."

"For twelve years I've known Amir. Twelve! Of course, they're good people. We're not strangers to each other you know. Everything will be fine, so stop with your worrying."

They were makin' their way up the elevator to the fifth floor before they knew it. Max waited a minute, standin' in the hallway in front of their door takin' in a deep breath.

"What are you doing Max?"

"I'm smelling. To find out what the food will taste like," he said hushed.

"You could be smelling the neighbor's cooking. Stop being a crazy person and ring the doorbell."

Amir was dressed up more than they had ever seen him before in a pressed shirt and tie.

"Welcome! Let me take your coats," he said. "Please come in."

Max helped Leah off with her coat, his nose still in the air sniffin'. She turned to thank Max for helpin' her and she gave him the evil eye, for still smellin' the air.

"Dinner's almost ready. Zara and I have been cooking since we got home. I left the store in the hands of my niece Kalila. My nephew is helping tonight too, but Kalila – she knows the business."

"I hope business is good for you this year," said Leah.

"It's been very busy, with so many people buying gifts for Christmas. Could I get you some wine while we wait?"

"No, thank you," said Max.

"It's kosher."

"Wine would be nice," said Leah, giving Max a look.

"Yes, wine would be nice," said Max.

"Please have a seat."

"Hello," said Zara, walkin' out of the kitchen. "Dinner's almost ready, so don't fill up. Here's some falafel and dip."

"We made everything kosher tonight. We did our best anyway. Putting Middle East politics aside," Amir said with a warm smile, "we chose dishes we thought we'd all enjoy."

"Amir made these himself," said Zara as she and Amir pulled up chairs to make a circle around the coffee table.

"Politics we shouldn't get into," said Leah. "We should pray that everyone could see love before anything else. Of course, we all celebrate our own holidays. Let's be glad we found a reason to be together."

"You're so right, Leah. We can make December twentieth *our* holiday. A day when similarities are celebrated," Zara said, raising her glass. "Let's call this day 'our holiday of peace'."

"Mozel Tov!" said Max.

"Happy holidays," said Zara. "May God bless peacemakers all over the world."

Their glasses touched each other that night, *and* their spirits. It wasn't the wine that put 'em at ease with each other, it was Leah and Zara talkin' about love that brought their hearts together. Love's what made 'em see the good in each other, and see all they had in common. The friendly conversation went on as they sat down to dinner.

"Something smells good!" declared Max.

Leah gave him a quick kick under the table when the others weren't lookin'.

"We have chicken with figs," Leah announced as she and Amir placed the platters before 'em, "roasted vegetables, potato kugel, and a few of Amir's specialties. Enjoy!"

"I love potato kugel. Are you sure you're not Jewish?" Max said jokin'.

"It's so nice of you to cook kosher for us," said Leah. "We were hoping to try some of *your* favorite foods."

"If that's what you want, then next time," said Amir. "I'm sure there'll be a next time!"

"Yes," said Max, "I'm sure they'll be a next time."

"I'm sorry to bring bad news," said Leah, "but since we're all together, I think we should talk about the children."

"Yes," said Max, "there's some very bad news about Sam."

"What happened? She isn't hurt, is she?" asked Zara.

"Sam's mother Grace, God rest her soul, passed away yesterday."

"Oh, no! That's terrible. How did you find out? Did Sam tell you?" asked Amir.

"Poet told me," said Max. "He heard it from Dadge."

"It was the life she lived," said Leah. "You know... on the street. Dadge said poor Sam doesn't have anyone to take care of her."

"There must be some relative. Isn't there an aunt or uncle who could take her in?" asked Zara.

"According to Poet," said Leah, "Grace left home when she was just a teenager because of abuse... The kind I shouldn't talk about at the table. From what Poet told us, Sam is better off if Grace's relatives stay out of the picture."

"It's not just Sam," said Max. "Pauly, the little boy, has been living with Sam in the apartment for three weeks now. He was abandoned by his own mother."

"We've been giving them plenty to eat; don't you worry. It's a shame they have no one. We don't know what's going to happen to those two darlings.

"How does Poet know so much about them?" asked Amir. "Does he take care of them?"

"It's his business," said Max. "He spends evenings on a certain corner every night selling drugs. Nothing too bad, according to Poet. There's a woman who works on the same corner, next to the liquor store, and she's friendly with Sam's mother – or I should say, was."

"And now, with Christmas coming so soon," said Leah, "that will only make things worse."

The talk soon rolled around to other things more fittin' to a get-together. What with them eatin' all that good food and havin' a good time gettin' to know each other, the ev'nin' flew by. Before they knew it, dinner was over.

"This is the coffee I told you about Leah. It doesn't taste

like coffee, but it's very good! Look at how fancy the coffee pot is."

"This was my mother's coffee pot," said Zara. "It's something I love. I wish I had a daughter I could leave it to."

"I pray God will bless you both," said Leah. "You'll make fine parents."

"This time we'll have some dates and candied fruit to go with our coffee," said Amir.

"And in a little while, we'll have chocolate cake," said Zara. "I made it myself. And don't worry... it's kosher!"

"Chocolate cake!" said Max.

"Max, you sound like you're five years old," Leah said.

"What can I say? I like chocolate cake."

Ev'rybody chuckled and went on with their coffee and dessert. They ate, talked about food, the way holidays were when they were kids, and the way their grandparents celebrated 'em. The Coens naturally ended up sittin' next to each other on one side of the dinner table, with Amir and Zara on the other. Somehow, the table in between 'em didn't divide 'em up at all. The warm hearts and generous spirits on both sides were brought together by the food in the middle.

It's pretty easy to look at other folks as family when you're breakin' bread with 'em. There was even a healthy portion of laughter now and then, to add to the flavor. By the end of the evening, both couples felt the same way. Outside might'a been freezin', but, inside, their warm hearts and warm smiles, made 'em feel like they were all family.

CHAPTER 19. GOIN' TO JAKE'S. ALMOST CHRISTMAS

It was just about Christmas day, and ev'ry kid that didn't have someone to care about 'em was talkin' about how Santa was gonna give 'em just what they wanted. I thought it was long overdue for me to pay a visit to Hi to see what was the chance of a thing like that actually happenin'.

Walkin' up to Jake's buildin' I noticed right away the front steps were decorated. There was fake evergreen wrapped around the iron railin's with ornaments hangin' on 'em. Two little Christmas trees in flower pots were settin' on each side of the door. An' each of the two wood doors had wreaths on 'em. I thought for sure Hi had done it all.

When I went inside, first thing I saw was Jake's door wide open. I thought he had been robbed or somethin', so I poked my head in slow and careful.

"Hi, Poet. You want some eggnog?"

Jake startled me when he said that – actin' like some kind'a jack-in-the-box, poppin' out at me.

"What!"

"I watched you walkin' up here. Do you want some eggnog?"

"What's your door doin' open? I thought somethin' happened to you! Don't you always keep this thing locked? The door only has five or six bolts on it."

"I've been takin' letters for Hi, and look," he said, motionin' with his chin. "Look at all the drawin's. The kids bring 'em here."

There were papers of kid's drawin's taped all over his place, in the hallway and leadin' up the stairs, windin' their way as far up as I could see. Pictures in crayon mostly, of Hi lookin' like Santa and pictures of Dancer as a reindeer. All dif'rent kinds and ways, but they were all about Hi somehow bein' Santa Claus.

"Look at what all the kids did! They bring more over every day. It's only three more days to Christmas, you know."

For the first time I remember, Jake had his TV off and he was playin' Christmas music on his radio.

"Have you lost your mind! What's wrong with you. You know how many disappointed, cryin' kids there gonna be on Christmas when they finally figure out the Santa Claus who lives in *your* buildin' is a phony?"

"Hi isn't a phony. The kids are gonna be happy. He's getting each one something they want."

"Have you gone into his apartment and seen what a mess of stuff he has in there? His place is full of a lot of broken up junk. You think kids are gonna be happy gettin' broken messed up junk for Christmas?"

"Listen, Poet, I want you to get out of here. The only reason you come around here is for kickbacks. Now you're criticizing a man who has a heart as big as this city, who only thinks about helpin' kids nobody else cares about! If you don't shut up about Hi, I'm gonna throw you out on your ass!"

"Jake, come to your senses. He's not thinkin' about the kids. He's only thinkin' about himself and how good it makes him feel *dreamin'* about helpin' kids."

"Go home, Poet! You're no model citizen, ya know. Go home and think about somebody besides yourself just this once."

"You're as crazy as he is! You wait 'til Christmas. You'll see what a mess he's made."

I left so angry I talked to myself for ten blocks.

"I don't care who hears me. So many crazy people around here, one more won't matter. I can't believe a real man like Jake goin' off the deep end like that. Eggnog and Christmas carols! Like he caught some kind'a sickness from Hi. What's the matter with people? I'm the only one who cares about the kids, not Hi."

My own words came back to me after I ended my rant. If I really cared about the kids, *I* would'a been the one tryin' to round up presents for 'em. A broken, old present would at least let a kid know somebody was thinkin' about 'em.

I saw myself in the glass of a store window. I had nothin' but a scowl. "Who am I to tell off Jake an' Hi. I'm just somebody nobody cares about. I'm not gettin' even a broken somethin', not for Christmas, and sure not for my birthday either. And I'll prob'ly be alone at my own funeral. I got nothin' to show for myself, and I'll be forgotten as soon as I'm gone. At least Hi's doin' somethin', even if it is makin' one big mess."

CHAPTER 20. VIC GETS A GUN. CHRISTMAS EVE

*I*t was a bitin' cold that ev'nin'. The two boys met under a streetlight with snow startin' to come down thick, with the wind blowin' it around in swirls, just like in a snow globe. This Christmas Eve started out as cruel as the weather.

"Hey, Dadge. Look!"

Vic pulled a gun from underneath his coat. Proud as a peacock he showed it off to Dadge.

"Where'd you get that?" asked Dadge.

"Jubba gave it to me."

"So that's yours now?" he asked, reachin' out.

"Almost. After I kill a guy. Then the gun's mine, and I'm in forever!"

"Kill somebody!" said Dadge, pullin' his hand back fast.

"That's the way you do it. After that, you can't ever turn on 'em 'cause they have somethin' on you. You gotta come with me. You're almost in."

"No way, Vic! I'm not gonna do that!"

"What's wrong with you? You'll be alone out there. Next thing you know, *you'll* be a target. You get in with Jubba's crew – then you'll have *fifty* guys to watch your back."

"I don't like the way those guys make me feel. They're always lookin' sideways at me. I don't trust them. And why should I have to kill somebody just to have some guys back me up?"

"The way you *feel*! Maybe you're not tough enough to make it. This isn't about feelings. This is your chance to be part of somethin'. Without us, you'll get crushed out there. Come on! You have to go in with me. We're family!"

"I didn't know that was part of the deal. I'm not gonna kill anybody! Who you gonna shoot anyway? Did they tell you that?"

"Yeah, they told me. I'm gonna kill that crazy old man who thinks he's Santa Claus – and I'm gonna shoot his dog, too!"

"You're the one who's crazy! Everybody'll hate you if you do that. He doesn't bother anybody, and he's gonna give presents out to all the kids."

"You believe that shit?"

"I don't know. I *do* know he didn't do anything to deserve getting shot."

"Jubba wants him dead, so he's gonna be dead. If it ain't me, it'll be somebody else. I'm gonna kill that old man. 'Cause when I do, I'm *in*. You comin' or what?"

"I have someplace else to go."

"Where you have to go that's more important than this?"

"I'm going to the Coens. I want to talk to them about Sam.

If I don't take care of Sam, she won't have anyone to watch out for her."

"So, what? She's not your sister. Or do you have a thing for her?"

"It's not like that. She's a little girl, and her mother's dead. She needs somebody."

"She'll be alright. Somebody'll take care of her. She'll go to foster care or somethin'."

"I'm *gonna* talk to the Coens. They'll know what to do."

"What'a you want to talk to them for? Those old people don't know shit."

"They care. Maybe they can think of something."

"They're not *your* people. They don't care about you. Jubba said, if I don't kill that old man, he's gonna ex *me* out. You watch yourself!" Vic said, pushin' Dadge's shoulders with both hands. "You snitch on me to those old people and Jubba will ex *you* out!" he said, pushin' Dadge real hard. "So, go, if you're gonna go!" Vic said, givin' one last, hard shove. Then he turned and walked away.

I make it a rule not to drink while I'm doin' biz'ness 'cause I have money to count. That night, I was savin' my drinkin' for later, knowin' I'd be alone on Christmas. There are folks I could scare up if wanted, but there wasn't anybody I felt close enough to, to ease up my loneliness. Fillin' loneliness with company is a tricky thing. Bein' around folks who think they should invite someone like me into their holidays 'cause I'm alone, makes me feel like a fifth wheel. If I'm with a tight family and I'm sittin' in on dinner, I feel like I'm standin' on the sidelines when ev'rybody else is in the game. But if the holidays are good for somethin', it's biz'ness.

On Christmas Eve, this old corner is almost as busy as Times Square itself. The liquor store does a heck of a biz'ness and so do the girls. Christmas Eve has always been the best night in the year for sellin' my product – better than New Year's Eve by far. There must be a lot of folks feel the same way I do. They'd rather be in their own company high or drinkin' than in the company of folks they don't really belong with. And they need somethin' to get 'em through, 'til they stop hearin' the words 'holiday' and 'family' bein' broadcast night and day. Connie's another one of us lonely people. She really loaded up this year. She bought four batches of rocks from me. She's never done that before.

"Connie, you gonna spend all your money with me tonight?"

"Might as well, Poet. I don't have anybody else to spend it on."

"You must have some family. Have any kids?"

"I have a daughter someplace. She'd be twenty-six by now."

"Don't you see her now and then?"

"I haven't seen her since I was fifteen. I gave her up for adoption. No way I could take care of her."

Connie was marchin' in place to keep warm. I felt like reachin' out to her to give her a hug, but I thought she'd take it wrong.

"I hope she turned out alright. Every once in a while, I go

into church and light a candle. It's something anyway. How about you? You alone?"

"I'm alone alright. I know I don't have any kids. I kept track. I have plenty of relatives though, but they're a worthless lot. Sometimes I think I was born in the wrong house."

Connie and me were too busy that ev'nin' to go on talkin'. On about eleven o'clock, I decided to pack it in. It's not my habit of walkin' around with a lot of cash, 'cause I don't want anybody thinkin' of me as a mark. I had raked in a wad by then, and things were slowin' down enough for me to call it a night. Big flakes of snow – twice a big as cornflakes, were comin' down fast and the wind was blowin' hard. Connie was out workin' more and more the later it got. There are lots of folks don't want to be alone on the holiday I guess – even if the company *is* temporary.

"Merry Christmas, Poet."

"Merry Christmas, Connie," I said as I was walkin' away.

I stopped in at the liquor store before headin' home. Lots of times it doesn't snow 'til January. A white Christmas always makes me feel good. I wasn't goin' out in it the next day anyway. There were red and green city decorations on the lamp posts. By ev'ry streetlight, the snow lit up bright against the night sky. Snow made the city feel clean, and decorations in the store windows cheered me up.

It didn't take long for Dadge to start thinkin' about what would happen if he didn't do anything and just let things go. He believed Vic when he said Jubba'd be after him for snitchin'. Snitchin's bad in anybody's book. But Dadge thought he'd break the rule this time 'cause Hi didn't deserve to get shot over nothin'. Hi hadn't done anything to bring this down on his head.

Dadge thought about what the right thing to do would be. He finally figured the Coens were too old to know what to do about somethin' that was hap'nin' on the street. So, Dadge made a bee-line for my place. He pounded on my door for a while and called for me. When I didn't come out, he went to my corner next.

"Poet! Poet!" Dadge yelled from a block away.

"Shut up!" Connie yelled back.

"Is Poet there?"

"Shut up Dadge! You're gonna chase away my trade."

"I have to talk to Poet right away. Is he around?" he asked as he got close to Connie.

"He left about fifteen, twenty minutes ago."

"Where'd he go? I have to talk to him."

"He said he was going home. I saw him duck into the liquor store. He's probably tying one on at *his* place."

"I have to do something. It's Vic. He's gonna shoot Hi – Mr. Engle."

"Who's Mr. Engle?"

"You know, the guy who thinks he's Santa Claus."

"Why would anybody shoot Santa Claus on Christmas Eve? Who would do somethin' like that?"

"It's Jubba. Jubba's told Vic he had to do it. I have to stop him. Tell Poet. We gotta do somethin' to stop him!"

"Don't be yelling about Jubba around here. Not unless you want to get your throat cut by one of his guys. Hey, where you going?" she yelled as Dadge took off down the street.

Dadge ran back to my place and started poundin' on the

door again. He didn't know that I had stopped off at a bar in the meantime. I couldn't wait to get a few drinks in me. It was easier to start drinkin' in a room full of folks than alone. Anybody seen me would'a thought I was celebratin' the holiday. I was only stallin' before I went back to my empty apartment to drink some more. After Dadge gave up, he left and went lookin' for Vic instead.

CHAPTER 21. CHRISTMAS MORNIN'

By Christmas mornin' the snow lay on the ground like new, white carpet. New fallen snow always makes a day seem extra peaceful to me. The quiet of it made it easier for me to sleep late. So, I was dreamin' deep when I heard somethin' at my window. Snowballs! Somebody was chuckin' snowballs at my window. 'Some damn kids,' I thought. A minute later, after I'd already drifted back to sleep, I heard knockin' at my door.

"Poet, it's me, Connie. Let me in."

I got up groggy from drinkin' and a little angry too. It was no kind'a day to be woken up early. I thought it must be somethin' important 'cause Connie never came up to my place before.

"What is it?" I asked through the door as I was gettin' up.

"Open the door. I have to talk to you."

I let her in without worryin' about how I looked, figurin'

she was used to seein' all kinds of men who just got out of bed.

"I had *some* night," she said and sat on the side of my bed. "I'm on way home now. I made a fortune. They were coming out in the dark and through the snow. I'm dead on my feet."

"Not that I mind but… What are you doin' here?"

"It's that kid. That friend of yours, Dadge. He said somebody was going to kill that guy you told me about, the crazy guy who thinks he's Santa Claus."

Right away, I started dressin'. I was trippin' over myself I was movin' so fast.

"When was that? When did he tell you that?"

"Last night. Not long after you left."

"Why didn't you tell me sooner?"

"Somebody's always saying they're gonna kill somebody around here. I hear that kind'a thing all the time. I just quit work so here I am. You think he's serious?"

"I gotta run!"

I left Connie sittin' there on my bed, while I ran out of the buildin'. Slipped on the snow I don't know how many times, makin' my way to Jake's apartment buildin'. I was pantin' and my lungs hurt from breathin' in all that cold air. The streets around Hi's apartment looked like the United Nations of kids. There were children of ev'ry description. There were plenty of rich kids there too, which puzzled me at the time. 'What would rich kids want with Hi's broken up, old toys?' I wondered.

There were a slew of kids in the alley, standin' in the snow lookin' up. Hi's window was wide open. Garland and decorations were all hangin' off the fire escape like they were thrown out of his window. There must'a been a ton of silver tinsel hangin' off the black-painted fire escape railin's.

"Hi, Poet!" I heard from down below.

It was little Pauly, lookin' up at me. He was holdin' hands with Sam.

"What happened?" I asked. "Did they find Hi? Has anybody called the police?"

"What for?" asked Sam.

"Look!" said Pauly, pointin' up at the open window while hangin' on to Half-a bear with the same hand. "Dancer turned into a reindeer and flew out the window with Santa!"

I looked around expectin' to see sad faces, but I didn't see a one. All the kids Hi made promises to were there, wide-eyed and happy, just like you'd expect kids to look at Christmas. Their hair might not'a been combed, and some of their clothes maybe didn't fit right, but they were the finest lookin' bunch of kids you'd ever want to see.

They stood there more than quiet, lookin' up at the open window and the decorations that were pourin' out over the fire escape. I'd say they were as quiet as if they were in a church.

"'S'cuse me, kids. I'm goin' upstairs to see what's goin' on."

I started walkin' – afraid of what I might find in Hi's apartment. I went inside the buildin' and knocked on Jake's door.

"Jake, you in there? Jake!"

It didn't take any time for Jake to come to the door.

"Poet, what are you doin' here?" he said.

"What happened last night? Was there a shootin'?"

"What are you talkin' about? Shootin'? Who shot who?"

"I heard somebody was out to shoot Hi. Did you hear anything?"

"Last night I thought I heard something. I was asleep, dreamin'. I heard reindeers on the roof. I swear I did. I woke up. But I went right back to sleep."

"Hi's window's open and a lot of his junk's been thrown out onto the fire escape. We better take a look."

We ran up the stairs as best we could: me out of breath and Jake, well, he just *couldn't* run. I tried tellin' him what I knew as we headed up.

"Word on the street said Vic was gonna shoot Hi. I just found out about it and ran right over as soon as I could. I hope it isn't true."

I got a horrible creep come up my backbone when I saw the door to Hi's apartment wasn't shut tight. If Jake wasn't there with me, I might not'a gone in.

"Hi. You in there?" I hollered as I opened up the door. "Hi?"

It was eight in the mornin' and made bright by the snow. I turned on the light anyway.

"Hi. You in here?"

Then, Jake called a few times. There wasn't a need to call much, since his place wasn't very big. We walked around checkin' all the rooms. With all Hi's junk around, it was hard to tell if the place had been ransacked or not.

"You know who all those kids are outside?" I asked Jake.

"They're kids who think Hi was – I mean – *is* Santa," he answered.

"*I* can tell you who they are. *Those* kids outside are all the kids Hi made promises to. I don't know what to say to 'em if they ask me where he is. 'Cause I don't know what happened myself!"

Jake thought a few seconds, and then he said, "I'll take care of it, Poet. I got this covered."

Jake climbed out the open window and stood on the fire escape announcin' to the kids like he was a dignitary or dictator maybe.

"Hey, kids! Santa Claus ain't here. He's gone to the North Pole and won't be back until next year. So go home. Merry Christmas! Hey Kwan it's me, Jake. Come around the front. I've got somethin' for you."

"Look at this here," I said, pickin' up that broken skateboard Hi found in the trash. "Look at this. Hi told me time and again he was gonna fix this up for Dadge. By the look of things, he hasn't fixed up one of these things. Those kids sure are gonna be disappointed."

I threw the broken board back on the pile of junk I found it on. Then Jake and I shut up the place and walked back downstairs.

"Who's Kwan?" I asked.

"He's one of the kids who visits Hi here sometimes."

"What's he got to do with you?" I asked as we kept walkin' down.

"We got to talkin' one day, and one thing led to another. So, I got him a present. I ain't bought a present for a kid in years!"

"Why'd you do it, Jake?"

"I felt like it, I guess. The kid reminds me of me when I was his age. He's pretty tough lookin', but I know he's just like all the other kids. He just wants somebody to be thinkin' about him once in a while."

"Somethin's happened to you."

"And another thing – I'm doublin' the kickbacks. If you ever find somebody else like Hi, you bring 'em right over, pronto! Understand?"

Jake was usin' his usual threatenin' soundin' voice, but he had turned into a marshmallow.

"I'll keep Hi's room for him for a while in case he comes back."

"I don't think he's comin' back."

"I got Kwan this computer game he wanted. He didn't ask for it; Hi told me he wanted it. I can't wait to see his face when he opens it!"

"Uncle Jake!" Kwan hollered when we saw him.

"So now you're an uncle?"

"Hey, Kwan. Santa left somethin' for you in my place. Come on in and see." Jake turned to me grinnin' like the Cheshire cat. "Merry Christmas, Poet. Come around later and we'll have some eggnog. I'll spike it for you."

"Jake, by the looks of things, I think you've had enough of your own eggnog already. I'll catch up with you."

The kids were all walkin' away when I got outside, 'cept for Sam and Pauly. They were waitin' for me.

"Is Mr. Engle gone, Poet?" Sam asked, with big sad eyes.

I didn't know what to say. No way was I was gonna mention that he was prob'ly shot dead in an alley somewhere.

"Yeah, he's gone, honey. You know how Santa is. He's got a

lot of work to do what with deliverin' presents to kids all over the world and all."

"Is he going to come back?" asked Pauly.

"I don't think so. I think he's done all he's ever gonna do around here – ever."

Sam tried hangin' her head, but Pauly's excitement made us both feel better.

"We gotta get our presents! I'm getting a bat, a ball, and a real baseball glove!"

"Now, just where do you think these presents ought'a be?" I asked, thinkin' I was goin' to have to let him down easy.

"At Mr. and Mrs. C's! I think," Pauly replied.

"I don't believe the Coen's *have* a Christmas tree. And the store's closed today anyway."

"We don't have a tree, too," Pauly said. "I bet our presents are at the store. Can we go, Sam?"

"Might as well. We don't have any place else to go. Will you come with us, Poet?" she asked, takin' hold of my hand. Pauly did likewise by gettin' hold of my other hand and then he started pullin'.

Those kids had my insides tied up in knots. I didn't want to be there when they found out there weren't any presents. Even more, I couldn't leave 'em so they'd be cryin' all alone either.

"Well, come on. We might as well all go, seein' as how none of us have any place to be today. Least we'll all be together."

So Pauly was pullin' me along with one hand, while Sam was holdin' my other hand. There I was in the middle, like some kind'a grandpa.

I hated to see the look in Sam's eyes. I could tell she was

havin' to grow up faster than her years, just like Dadge had. She looked sad worryin', while Pauly was so excited about what he'd find at the Coen's. He pointed and smiled at decorations and threw snowballs at telephone poles the whole way there. He even sang "Jingle Bells" a couple times. By the look of him on this day, nobody would ever see him for what he really was: an unwanted kid.

By the time we got close to Coen's Deli, Pauly had cheered us all up. I could see the dark behind Coen's window from half a block away. But there was Amir, outside, shovelin' the sidewalk around the stores.

"Sam! Pauly!" he yelled.

He threw his shovel aside and got down on one knee. He had his arms out like the kids should run to him.

"Children, Merry Christmas!" he said all cheerful.

The two ran up to him, but they stood out of his reach. Amir knelt on both knees while talkin' to 'em real soft.

"Sam and Pauly, I was hoping to see you here today. Something strange has happened. Santa left presents for both of you under the tree at our house."

"Really?" asked Sam.

"Yes. Packages wrapped in holiday paper with red ribbons and bows addressed to each of you."

"I told you!" Pauly yelled, lookin' up at me. Then he turned to Sam, "I told you so!"

"Wouldn't you like to come to our home to open up your presents?" he asked real kind.

"We sure would," said Sam with a happy grin. "Wouldn't we, Pauly?"

"We sure would!"

"I don't know when I can bring you back. You'll probably have to stay for Christmas dinner and pie. I hope you don't mind."

"I'm so hungry, I'll eat the whole pie!" said Pauly.

"Why don't you come along, Poet. I think Santa left something for you too."

"Thanks, Amir. That's real kind of you, but you take care of the kids.'

"You have to come," said Sam, hangin' on my arm. "Have to!"

"Yeah," said Pauly, tuggin' on my other arm and holdin' up his bear. "Half-a Bear wants you to come!"

"Well...it's hard to say no to Half-a Bear. And seein' how Santa left a present for me, I'll have to come along to find out what it is."

"Come on," said Amir. "We'll all go. There are presents for everyone and plenty to eat. We'll all have a Merry Christmas *together*!"

CHAPTER 22. WRAPPIN' IT UP

urns out Santa left me a long, wool scarf at Amir's. Considerin' that this was the first Christmas tree Amir and Zara ever had, it's pretty amazin' there was such a good crop of gifts underneath. Pauly got that baseball stuff he'd been promised, and it was all brand new. And Sam got a warm, winter jacket after all.

That was a special Christmas, 'cause it wasn't anything about presents. It was about ev'rybody comin' together and figurin' out who their real families were. 'Cause that year, children *and* grown-ups got all the love they ever wanted. Once those two children went into the house, they never did leave. Amir and Zara started proceedin's right away. They took in Pauly and Sam in as foster children 'til they could adopt 'em both. Even Half-a Bear got adopted. He got washed, stuffed, and put up on a shelf all his own. The Coens spent their first Christmas with Amir and Zara, too, as the unofficial adopted grandparents of Pauly and Sam.

It went that way all over the city. Folks who had love to give gave to ev'ry child in need. So, all the children Hi made promises to got that one special thing they wanted – people to care about 'em. I went all around the city tryin' to find somebody Hi scammed, visitin' ev'rybody I knew. There wasn't one disappointed child Hi had made promises to and nobody had given their money away to Hi.

It was well after Christmas that we were all gettin' worried about Dadge. Nobody had seen him or Vic for three weeks. We were all prayin' for 'em – even me. Then, about two weeks after the New Year, there was Dadge, standin' in the doorway of Coen's Deli.

"Dadge!" Leah yelled out. "Max, Dadge is back. Look!"

"Dadge! You're back!" Max yelled.

"We're so happy to see you, bubala!" Leah yelled, throwin' her arms around him and layin' a big kiss on his cheek. "It's so good to see you."

"We all missed you," said Max, throwin' his arm around Dadge's shoulder, givin' him a sideways hug. "Believe it or not Santa left a present for you here in the back of our store. You'd be surprised! This year Santa Claus visited more people than you can imagine. You know, we need someone we can trust around here. I think maybe you could be a manager, but, of course, you'll have to start out on the slicer," Max said all happy and excited. "We'll get to that later. For now, I'm going to make us both, two nice, thick ham sandwiches!"

"But Mr. C., I thought you didn't eat ham."

"Of course, I eat ham. Who doesn't like ham? We'll eat it in the back. That's what I always do," he said hushed. "So long as nobody sees, it's alright!"

Max led him into the back room. Dadge spotted his present leanin' up in the corner. It was easy to tell by the shape of it what it was. He felt good walkin' next to Max. So instead of runnin' over to get his present, he stuck right by Max's side. Whatever happened to Dadge while he was away, it made him grow up older than his years – in a good way. Somehow, a skateboard didn't seem so important anymore. He knew, belongin' with folks who cared about him was so much better.

Turns out, Vic and Hi both disappeared Christmas Eve. Word on the street was that when Vic went to Hi's to ex him out, the old man and his dog were already gone. So, Vic ran off so Jubba couldn't ex *him* out. Vic hasn't been heard from since. Seems he was about the only one in town who didn't get what he wanted.

Nobody ever did figure out where Hi and Dancer got to. The children all believe they went to the North Pole. I'm of the opinion they prob'ly went someplace even higher up than that.

I don't think Hi *was* Santa Claus. I think he might'a been an angel though. If he *was* an angel, I think he might'a been the most cleverest angel who ever come to earth to do a good deed. 'Cause, he'd figured out a way for all kinds of folks to be generous without anybody even havin' to ask 'em to. Just for bein' the kind'a man he was, he made ev'rybody around him feel like givin'. Hi never asked anything for himself. All's he did was to go around thinkin' about children and what they needed most.

I got what I needed most, too. I got recruited! Just like soft-hearted Jake, I started to care. Imagine me, gettin' somethin' *I* needed for Christmas, a good feelin' inside, just like all those children. Now I see the whole world in a dif'rent way.

I see it like this. At Christmas time, when it snows, some folks only see all that snow piled up, and think about the weight of it. Then there are folks who see the flakes come down one at a time and think how each one makes the world a little more beautiful. That's the way I see all the children nobody seems to care about. It's hard to think about the weight of 'em all – how hard it is to feed 'em all or spend the time to make each one feel special. So, I think of 'em one at a time, knowin' that each one is beautiful.

Now, ev'ry year *I* look for flowers that grow up in between the cracks of the sidewalk; whether they're real flowers, or whether they're a new crop of children. We have to be careful with 'em and be sure to walk softly around 'em so we don't tramp out their spirits.

I wonder how many folks pray when they want somethin'? All of 'em I expect. But *who ever* prays to God to help an angel do *his* work? Nobody I expect. I know *one* angel who could'a used some prayers to help him along. So, on that Christmas, I made up my mind right there and then, to help the next angel by doin' the same kind'a work they'd do.

I came to my senses and stopped selling drugs. I came to see they were hurtin' the people I was sellin' to. And, I stopped pan-handlin', and went out and got a job. Can you imagine me workin' regular? Jake and I decided his buildin' could use a good bit of fixin' up. Turns out I'm a pretty good handyman. Jake gave me one of his apartments to live in. He said I can stay here forever if I want to. I feel good now that I've grown roots. My place feels like a real home – 'specially wakin' up to Connie right next to me ev'ry mornin'. Home! I have a home!

I'm a changed man 'cause of Hi. I found out Christmas isn't about givin' toys at all. It's all about givin' love. So, now *I'm* the one thinkin' about the children. If I have somethin' to give, I get 'em a present for their birthday or Christmas. If I don't have any extra to buy 'em a warm coat, or a baseball glove, I give 'em a smile or take time to listen.

I think it's hard bein' an angel – tryin' to do good in a hard world with no one to thank you. Now *I* pray for all the angels that give water to a stray dog. I pray for the angels that think about the children; that give 'em food for their hungry mouths and love for their hungry hearts. And I pray for myself. "God, let me be that kind of angel, too sometimes."

Made in the USA
Las Vegas, NV
23 November 2022

60032706R00102